KU-641-476

RENEGADE PREACHER

DM

Warwickshire County Council

KCS 7/16

BI

02 SEP 2022

21 NOV 2018

This item is to be returned or renewed before the latest date above. It may be borrowed for a further period if not in demand. **To renew your books:**

- **Phone the 24/7 Renewal Line 01926 499273 or**
- **Visit www.warwickshire.gov.uk/libraries**

Discover • Imagine • Learn • *with libraries*

Warwickshire County Council

Working for Warwickshire

0135726524

Wh

girl

to

dec

By

to

con

tog

letl

un

thv

staying together seemed an important...

RENEGADE PREACHER

by

Syd Kingston

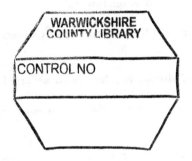

WARWICKSHIRE COUNTY LIBRARY

CONTROL NO

Dales Large Print Books
Long Preston, North Yorkshire,
England.

British Library Cataloguing in Publication Data.

Kingston, Syd
   Renegade preacher.

   A catalogue record for this book is
   available from the British Library

   ISBN 1-85389-981-X pbk

First published in Great Britain by Robert Hale Ltd., 1985

Copyright © 1985 by Syd Kingston

Cover illustration © FABA by arrangement with Norma
Editorial S.A.

The moral right of the author has been asserted

Published in Large Print 2000 by arrangement with Mrs
V. Bingley

All rights reserved. No part of this publication may be
reproduced, stored in a retrieval system, or transmitted in any
form or by any means, electronic, mechanical, photocopying,
recording or otherwise, without the prior permission of the
Copyright owner.

Dales Large Print is an imprint of
Library Magna Books Ltd.
Printed and bound in Great Britain by
T.J. International Ltd., Cornwall, PL28 8RW.

ONE

In one of the back rooms of the South-Western Traders' store, Wil Coltman surveyed his profile in a dusty wall mirror which had lost its silver backing in places. He was wearing a dark business suit as befitted a new, up-and-coming business house manager in a prosperous county such as Hot Springs, New Mexico territory.

This store, the one he had become probationary manager of some three months earlier, had been a talking-point among the worthies of the town of Clearwater over the past few weeks, in fact since the previous visit of George D Masters the general manager of the county chain of stores.

Two nights earlier, the town's current mayor, Frank S Thorne, a tight-fisted long-term resident and the number one saddler, had taken him aside in a saloon and actually bought him a small glass of whisky.

'Wilbur, laddie, you have the makings,' Thorne had said, rolling his Scottish consonants like a muted rattlesnake. 'Stay around long enough an' you could become a councillor, yoursel'!'

Wil had enjoyed the whisky and improved his local standing by buying the next round, but the mayor's seemingly prophetic words had left him feeling despondent instead of elated.

Wil nodded at his reflection without enthusiasm. Around the time when he had drifted westward into Hot Springs county, he had allowed his lush fair hair to grow long and acquired upon his usual clean-shaven face a long becoming fair beard and a luxuriant moustache which appeared to broaden his face.

He was affluent-looking, distinguished even, but he knew that the image he was presenting to the public was not really that of his father's son. Wilbur Bollard still lurked there behind the hirsute disguise. The blue eyes and the quizzical smile were still part of his new personality, and yet he knew he was not really cut out to be a shopkeeper.

Wil sniffed and rolled the half-smoked small cigar around from one side of his mouth to the other. Perhaps the few white hairs, nestling unseen in his sideburns linked the old Wil Bollard with the new Wilbur Coltman. Maybe today was a time to take stock. Not of the goods in the store he managed, but of himself, his present circumstances and his future. And his feelings on the matter.

He blinked a few times, paced up and down, and knew the depression was still there: the sinking feeling which he had experienced on and off ever since his meeting in the saloon with the mayor.

'Mr Coltman, can you spare a minute?'

The voice which summoned him belonged to Merle Brisson, his female

9

assistant, a hard-working widow of forty-two years with a lined face and greying hair who admired him intensely.

'Coming Mrs Brisson. Coming right away.'

He rubbed out the butt of his cigar, squared off his shoulders and strode purposefully into the shop. A farmer with a vast stomach under a buckskin tunic wanted to buy some Indian blankets for his wife's fortieth birthday. Wil put on his special smile, his becoming manner and used Mrs Brisson and young Carlos as foils as he put over his own personality and made a useful sale.

As soon as the customer had departed, Wil glanced at his pocket watch and came to a decision.

'Today, my good workers, we will lock up shop for siesta a little earlier than usual. I want the two of you to take lunch with me at Jack's Diner. Are you willing?'

Mrs Brisson blushed and almost curt-seyed, while young Carlos nodded and produced a smile which bisected his full sallow face from ear to ear.

Over the meal, Wil chatted up his two energetic and essential assistants. His words further boosted the uplifting feeling produced by the excellent food, and then he dropped his small surprise.

'It's over three months since I took over. Mr Masters promised to be in touch with me before twelve weeks had elapsed. I propose to hire a buckboard an' make a trip over to Newell to see him this very afternoon. I have so much confidence in you two that I may even stay in Newell overnight. Do either of you have any doubts about bein' able to cope in my absence?'

Merle Brisson delicately dabbed her mouth with a napkin before shaking her head quite firmly. Carlos deliberately slowed down his consumption of roast beef to refute such a suggestion with dignity.

'All right then, if you're sure,' Wil summed up. 'We can say our farewells right here an' now.'

He kissed the back of Merle's hand and bestowed upon Carlos a firm handshake which was well received. Twenty minutes later, he had changed, acquired the shaft-horse and buckboard and was driving past the store he managed when his female assistant darted into the dirt of the street off the sidewalk and waved a letter at him. Wil braked and caused the flighty shaft-horse to swerve.

A frown settled on his face. He was thinking his little trip was about to be curtailed. 'What is it, Merle?'

'A letter from back east, Mr Coltman! It only came in on the coach a few minutes ago. I didn't want you to miss it, sir! It's addressed to you. I hope it's good news. *Hasta la vista!*'

Merle beamed, flashing her gapped and ill-assorted teeth. The way she yearned after Wil was almost pathetic. And yet he knew her value as a shop assistant, and so he played up to her. On this occasion, he half rose in his seat, raised and waved his hat at her and caused a lot of heads to turn in order to see who he was communicating with.

As soon as the conveyance had turned a corner, he stuffed the letter into his pocket and concentrated upon getting well clear of town before the lethargy of siesta-time took charge of him. For a mile or so, the slight breeze created by his speed of travel did all he could have hoped for in that direction.

Perhaps a half-hour later, it occurred to him that Merle Brisson knew his real name, Wilbur Bollard. It was there, plainly written on the letter for anyone to see. He reflected upon the guile he had used to make the mail clerk believe that he had once acted on the stage as one Wilbur Bollard. And yet, his subterfuge was not so very far from the truth.

Maybe Merle did not know much about old Bollard country and associations linked with Bitter Creek and the old Circle B ranch. Time would tell.

From Clearwater to Newell was a distance by trail of about eight miles. In fact, it was the shortest distance between any two of the six towns in Hot Springs county.

Others had been active about the time when Wil made his move to close the South-Western Traders' store early. A trio who preyed upon lone travellers between towns duly noted the shopkeeper's sudden abandonment of routine and put it down to something connected with greed and gain. He was up to something, so they decided. Perhaps making off with the stores' takings. How was that for a guess?

They waited until he was safely started upon the short route to Newell (the name of which was a shortened form of New Well) and then they gave chase. Sonora, a Mexican-Indian, possessed the fastest riding horse and the most trail cunning. He, it was, who made a calculated detour in order to get ahead of the quarry so as to bring about his downfall.

Others had suffered due to the scheme they were carrying out this day, but no one had ever pinned any of the blame on them because the victims had all been killed and their bodies disposed of with infinite care.

It was almost three in the afternoon when the half-breed emerged from the heavy undergrowth on the north side of the trail and cautiously approached the vital spot where tall mature pine trees made an avenue of sorts out of the narrowest part of the seldom-used track.

For nearly two miles, Wil Coltman had dozed in his seat, swaying from side to side and blinking fitfully when the buckboard went over a stone or a wheel squealed over small rocks. After a time, he blinked as a course of treatment, attempting to make himself stay awake. It was while he was working his way through this routine that the first intimation that others were on the trail behind him came to his notice.

At first, there was only the distant jingle of harness. And then, after a short interval, he heard hoarse voices apparently raised in argument. A second clamour of voices made him suspicious. He dropped a hand on his right-handed .45 Colt, and later groped under the seat in search of a Winchester repeating rifle.

His mind was not at all clear about the exact amount of time since he had last made serious use of firearms.

Less than a furlong in the rear, the two quarrelsome riders slanged each other as the excitement of the chase boosted their pulse rates. The older man, a fleshy muscular character dabbed away perspiration from his jowl and brow, revealing as he lifted his stained stetson a crown of thinning sandy hair which was turning grey. He looked his forty-odd years of age.

Riding alongside of him, and slightly too close for comfort, a redheaded youth half the other's age showed his buck teeth in a grimace of displeasure. He rowelled the flanks of his round-barrelled veteran roan in an effort to outdistance his partner's racy buckskin.

'I don't like it, Red. You an' me always hangin' back, leavin' the real work to Sonora! That breed an' his knife! Huh, he thinks he can operate without the two of us, an' pretty soon he'll be right!'

'For cryin' out loud, be patient, Tommy! Sonora is good with his knife. You know that. Besides, if anything goes wrong he gets it, not us!'

The young man shook a fist at him. 'It ain't healthy, firin' off practise shots, an' never blastin' away in anger! And another thing I don't like, either! Me, I can ride as well as the two of you. But do I get to ride a spirited mount any time? No, I don't! Sonora gets the flyer an' *I* get the crowbait! So, I'm sickened. I need action, the real thing. *Vamos,* hoss!'

Having made it clear how he felt, the

younger rider set about his sweating horse as if a tribe of hostiles was rapidly catching them up in the rear.

Wil Coltman was perspiring, too. He had taken off his jacket and discarded the cream side-rolled stetson before stretching out under the seat, facing towards the rear. His hastily lighted cigar wobbled between his lips and added smoke to the dust which bothered his eyes a little.

The Winchester .73 was a well-balanced weapon. He hoped he would put it to some good use before the trail broadened again and started to meander. He glanced upwards, gauging the distance between the pine trees on either side of the track. Just when he was anticipating his first glimpse of the continuing pursuit, something flashed by overhead and startled him. There was a sudden flutter of wings, but it was not the bird. A perfectly straight line, parallel with the surface of the track! It was a lariat, stretched across the narrow trail, meant to knock him out of the seat, or to decapitate him!

'Hell an' tarnation,' he muttered, as the cigar dropped from his mouth, 'that there lariat ain't a nice weapon! These hombres act real mean!'

Another hundred yards further on, he contrived to slip out from his position over the tail. The cigar was back between his teeth when he managed to check the willing grey and apply the brakes. Anger added to his agility. He sprang to the ground with the Winchester, hastily found a spot between two rocks on the west side of the trail, and tested his sighting distantly upon a slight bend.

A long ninety seconds went by before the sounds of hooves built up sufficiently to confirm the closeness of the pursuit. The bulky roan headed the buckskin into view, swinging wide with its rider's legs prominent in a wide fork. Wil manoeuvred the cigar and its attendant smoke away from his left eye and made adjustments to his weapon. At the same time, he became aware of the second, more bulky rider coming through the fresh dust with a wolfish expression on his face.

Excitement made the ambusher blast off a second or two before he was truly settled. His first bullet hit the brim of the stiff headgear worn by the younger man. The hat went away like a flying disc. Two startled shouts blurred into each other. The second shot missed between the buckskin's neck and the saddlehorn.

The second rider lurched and grabbed for his stetson. 'Take cover, Tom! Jump for it!'

Wil kept firing then, as fast as he could lever. Chips of rock flew all over the disgruntled riders as they left leather and hurled themselves into rock cover. Some thirty seconds later, they started to fire back, one located on either side of the trail. Wil shared his favours. He reloaded his weapon, ignoring the probing return bullets. He was thoroughly absorbed in what he was doing, and levering for the third time, second round when a disturbing thought penetrated his concentration.

The two men who were his targets could not have set the lariat in place. That meant another man, or men, was lurking somewhere near by. Possibly quite close, behind a tree-bole. At once, his confidence began to ebb. He turned his attention to the trees and foliage near at hand. Defensive thinking had taken over. He grew breathless as he measured the distance between himself and the buckboard.

Blinking consistently with the stone chips flying around him, he counted up to five before getting to his knees and moving off, backwards, keeping his head and shoulders as low as possible without losing his balance. His nerves began to jump. There was a lull in the shooting. Fortunately, the shaft-horse—although it was steaming and thirsty—wanted to be on the move again.

He was breathing like a runner at the

end of a race. The brake reacted to his twitching hand, and then released the wheel. Two shots probed his new position as he coaxed the quadrupled into action with a hoarse cry. Horse and board jerked away. Wil lost his balance, but recovered again as he sat down hard.

Even then, with the wheels turning nicely under him, he still feared a bullet from someone who—as yet—had not shown where he was. Yard by yard, the troubled traveller drew away from the critical spot. No more bullets flew. Instead, there were muted distant cries, as if his attackers were comparing notes and trying to find out what had gone wrong.

Very gradually, the knotted muscles in his back began to relax. They would have stayed taut for much longer if he had known how close the lariat rigger was. Sonora was scarcely ten yards distant by the time the buckboard got under way, and he had been sorely tempted to use his Bowie-style knife for throwing purposes, instead of as a dagger.

Hatred caused by differences of opinion between the Indo-Mexican and his two white partners prevented the former from eliminating the intended victim with a strong throw. There would be other times, other victims. He was still in funds. As for his accomplices, they would be frustrated, bad tempered. He liked to contemplate them when they were ill at ease.

He started to make his way back to retrieve the lariat.

TWO

For perhaps twenty minutes after the restart, Wil bristled with anger. He had his confidence back and he wanted to protest to somebody about the vulnerability of a lone traveller on one of Hot Springs County's oldest trails.

Maybe he ought to go up to the peace office and complain to the town marshal: tell the fellow he ought to drum up a posse and flush out the villains who had resorted to ambushing to make a living. If the marshal argued, Wil could argue, too. He could ask how many travellers had vanished without trace in recent times between Clearwater and Newell. Such a question would take the wind out of an angry badge toter, but it might not force the fellow to swear out a posse.

Newell was distantly visible by the time Wil began to have his doubts about such a course of action. After all, posses between towns were the business of county sheriffs, and this county's seat was at Cheyenne Wells, over in the north-east. A long way off.

Perhaps if he just knocked on the door, stepped inside and reported the incident, in case other travellers suffered in the same way. Would that do? After all, he was unmarked and unhurt. Only his pride had suffered. So, what the hell? He would tell the marshal if he happened to see him.

George Masters was the hombre he was travelling to see. And even now, he was not so sure as to why he had quit Clearwater in such a hurry to have this manager person's opinion of him. Had he really been running away from his successful worthwhile backwater shopkeeping job? Or was it just restlessness? One thing was clear, he had not come this far in siesta-time merely for a pat on the back.

Newell had a hot, neglected, deserted look about it. Peeling paintwork, worn sidewalk boards and warped roofing timbers drew the attention of the latest visitor. No town in the west really welcomed a newcomer at this hour of the day. It was better to arrive after dark. The peace office had a blind masking the window. So did many of the shops. Some buildings were shuttered, and, to all intents and purposes, uninhabited. Wil Coltman yawned. He wondered if it was a good idea to tell George Masters, the worthy general manager of South-Western Traders, that he had held down the temporary manager's job in Clearwater using an assumed name.

Better wait till Masters had seen his sheets of figures before doing anything so drastic. Wil shrugged, and yawned again. He turned off Main Street down an intersection, knowing that the shops and houses on Second Street were in a far better state than on Main.

Masters' shop was the biggest in the

chain. It had a double frontage, and behind the glass windows lightweight lace curtains were drawn. The recessed door had a closed notice showing through the glass. At the rear, on the gallery, a newer more recent notice said, *'Please call later, Mr Masters is otherwise engaged.'*

Totally frustrated, Wil threw back his head and yawned. Only a cat, a dog and a man reclining in a hammock-style swinging divan saw him. He then drove on to the end of Second, and was fortunate enough to find a negro livery hand still awake. Between them, they manoeuvred the buckboard round the back and put the horse in a stall.

After that, the traveller took a bath, drank two pints of beer and sauntered back to the rear gallery behind the shop. There, he stretched out in a wicker chair and drew from his pocket the letter which had come into his possession just as he left Clearwater. It was from Clem Bollard, his father's surviving brother, in Philadelphia.

The envelope was addressed in ink, in a nicely rounded hand which made Wil frown in a puzzled fashion.

He began to read.

Spruce Villa
Woodside Park,
Philadelphia,
Penns.

Dear Wilbur,

I'm addressing this to you although us folks still in the east have no special notion of your doings or whereabouts.

We're all sad about the death of that dear wilful restless brother of mine, Henry, (the other year) and we feel guilty because none of us made the journey out west at the time of his funeral.

Let it be known that the telegraph message took three weeks to reach us. By then, Henry would have been interred, or 'planted' as you westerners like to say.

Kindly let us know exactly where he is laid to rest. We would like to know details of how you two surviving Bollards, Henry's sons, are getting on. Now and again, we have heard rumours through travelling folk that Henry's big cattle ranch is no more: that the land has passed to strangers. We hope this is untrue, and that peculiar notions about the cattle creek having been poisoned by chemicals or some such is also untrue.

What sort of men would pollute the water? Eh? Rumours suggest that our old rivals from the Old Country, the Grunbaums, have grown stinking rich in Hot Springs County, on account of that section of railroad, South Loop, which old Cy managed to organise. Cyrus' father was also a man for cutting corners!

We hope your Pa did not have to back down or anything due to the railway running across Bollard territory.

In case you feel the Grunbaums are getting too much of the limelight, we can tell you that the older son, Homer, isn't becoming a millionaire back here on the east coast. Matter of fact, he's in jail for embezzlement! How's that for a skeleton in the Grunbaum cupboard?

The old branches of the family in Pennsylvania have been steadily thinning out. It's all very sad. One lot went back to the Old Country, seven or eight others have died of old age, in this decade. And illness has taken care of three more.

Your cousin, Bella, is writing this down for me, and she's chesty. She could do with a spell out west in New Mexico's dry atmosphere. Which reminds me to ask after Miriam and Lettie Rodwell. If they're well, sound them out about a visit from Bella. It would be doing all the family a favour, if they'd take her for a while.

I'm kind of running out of ideas, somewhat, but cousin Bella might be able to add a thing or two. Meantime, we all send our love and best wishes and hope to hear good news from you real soon.

Affectionately yours,

Uncle Clem and cousin Bella.

P.S. We almost forgot to mention Clinton Mayer's daughter, Charleen. She is, of course, included in our good wishes.

P.P.S. It occurs to us that if either you or Rich has married her she will now be a Bollard niece, and a cousin! Adios.

Wil read through the letter without stopping. His breathing was shallow, all the way through the wordy epistle. His emotions stirred within him as the words of his uncle pinned down all the shortcomings of himself and the younger brother he had been supposed to care for.

How could he write and tell an old man like Clem of his wasted youth? How he had frittered away Henry's funds, mishandled his cattle and business, and turned to drink when the gambling had decimated the Bollard fortune?

How could he tell Uncle Clem how he had sold the Bollard acres to a family of travelling sheep farmers, expecting the poisoned creek waters to wipe out their

31

flocks and leave them with nothing to fatten on but thinning yellowed grass? He dropped the letter on the light circular table, and clutched his head as he thought of the greatest humiliation of all.

He started to mutter to himself, through his teeth.

'How was I to know the poison would gradually leave the creek, that the sheep herders would be allowed to stay, and that they would prosper on Bollard soil? How could the local folks despise the Bollard boys and tolerate ordinary Mexican sheep herders in the midst of cattle country?'

He ground his teeth, and eventually desisted. His spirits hit rock-bottom. He felt he was neither a slick salesman nor a western pioneer. His newly formed set of values seemed to amount to nothing. One thing was certain. He was tired. He left the wicker chair, and stretched himself out on a padded bench at the rear side of the gallery. In spite of his troubled thoughts, he soon slept.

George Masters, general manager of South-Western Traders, was a widower. He had fought in the Civil War, acquired a painful hip wound and a permanent limp. At fifty-five, the pain seemed to affect him more than when he was younger. In fact, that very morning he had banged his hip against a counter and sent an excruciating pain through his pelvis which had almost made him vomit.

Consequently, when the time came to close up for midday, he ate less than usual and drank a few tots of whisky in the hope of deadening the pain. The pain had responded somewhat, but failed to leave him altogether. His next move had been to visit his foremost female acquaintance, Dolores Smith. Dolores was the thirty-six-year-old widow of the late Doctor Cedric Smith. She was a smart, upstanding brunette with a lively mind, who had learned from her husband a number of useful skills for dealing with everyday complaints and some of the more common illnesses.

There was another doctor in the town, of course, and Dolores in no way cut across his patients or sought to be in competition, but the real sawbones was overworked, and everyone in town knew of Dolores' capabilities. So, she had visitors who needed a bit of timely help: especially those with aches and pains. Even in her husband's time, she had been a good masseuse.

Any other woman, taking in men and giving them a good pummelling would have occasioned adverse comment, but not Dolores: not even when it was known that in one or two cases her attentions went a little beyond the professional.

George Masters was a lean, attractive fellow with good manners, superb mixing ability and a reasonable education. The grey hairs in his thick wavy black mane and lush moustache did not detract from his youthful appearance.

George had been attracted to Dolores for a long time. In the previous twelve months, he had firmly believed that he meant more to her than her two or three other regular male 'patients'. Nothing in Dolores' attitude had led him to believe otherwise. At least, not until this particular day when some consideration not known to George had cut across their free and easy camaraderie and made her slightly impatient with him. It might have been the liquor he had drunk, or some other obvious consideration, but he had left her again without discovering what it was.

The return walk across town had sapped his energy and made him entertain pessimistic thoughts. Was it possible, for instance, that Dolores had taken a greater liking to one of her other male visitors, that she was tiring of him? Was it his own fault? Had he been less than explicit in making known his special feelings for her when opportunities had presented themselves?

Anger boosted his tired limbs. He began

to put down his feet more firmly, and that aggravated his weak hip again. By the time he reached the gallery at the back of the shop, he was feeling really sorry for his earlier intake of whisky, he was beginning to think he needed more. He started to calculate how many years had elapsed since he had acquired his wound. His face was a mask of concentration before he had finished, and then something distracted him and he declined to calculate further.

His distraction was the recumbent sleeping form of Wil Coltman. At first, George frowned. Why was Coltman sleeping here, taking life easy, when he ought to have been in Clearwater eight miles away, patiently getting ready to open up his branch of the stores and make himself agreeable to customers?

George's pulse gradually eased down. Wil would not be here without a reason. Wil was a good fellow. The best prospect as a branch manager in five years. George yawned. If nothing had gone wrong in

Clearwater, perhaps today was as good a day as any other to drink a friendly glass of liquor with this young man.

He needed male company. A confidant.

Under his ardent gaze, Wil Coltman stirred. Wil rocked his shoulders, came up into a sitting position, punched out the high-crowned cream-coloured side-rolled stetson which he was using for the trip and adjusted the knot of his black bandanna over his creased grey shirt.

He grinned. 'Hope I'm not puttin' you out by turnin' up like this unexpectedly, Mr Masters? I just had this restless feelin' an' I had to go somewhere. A visit to you at the time seemed the best thing to do, seein' as how I wanted to put our tradin' figures before you as soon as possible.'

Wil rose, and the two men shook hands. The hard lines of Masters' face suddenly relaxed, as he let out a gusty laugh. Wil was surprised to notice that his boss had been imbibing strong liquor. Up until this time he had thought Masters did not indulge in whisky. Maybe this was a special day for both of them.

Masters patted his visitor on the shoulder. 'I guess you did right to come, at that, Wilbur. Just so long as everything is runnin' along smoothly back in Clearwater.'

Wil gave him the assurances he needed, and handed over two sheets of figures and totals which gave a clear indication of the Clearwater shop's turnover and profits for the previous month. In spite of his weariness and general lack of enthusiasm, George Masters showed pleasure.

'All right, Wilbur, I'll give my full attention to these papers right away. Why don't you step into the building, wash up, an' collect the medicinal whisky from my office while I'm busy? I guess we'll have something to celebrate, huh?'

Wil fell in with Masters' instructions. As he washed himself, stripped to the waist, he reflected upon his liquor problem of a few months ago. Would a few drinks lead to the old craving for whisky which had done him a lot of harm in the past?

This day was going to be a testing one, in addition to his recent troubles on trail.

THREE

The exchanges over the Clearwater shop's trading were short and to the point. George Masters was very pleased. He found time to enthuse over the other shops in the South-Western Traders chain, and then—quite gradually—his spirits fell flat again.

Wilbur had seen to the pouring out of the whisky and, more to protect himself than any other consideration, he had weakened his own drinks by adding a finger or so of cordial to the potent liquor.

Masters clinked glasses with him at the first refill.

'Say, Wil, you're a bit of a dark horse in some respects. You aren't thinking of getting married, or anything, are you? Seems to me you have a spritely widow on your staff who might become interested in you.'

Wil shook his head and made negative signs with his cigar. 'Nope, nothin' like that in the near future, George. I—er—I had a long letter from kinsfolk back east, as a matter of fact. The clan is thinnin' out. Ain't much I can do about it, of course. But it did leave me feelin' rather low-spirited, I must admit. I find myself wonderin' if you could see your way to me havin' a day or two off. Don't want to go far. Merely a matter of thinkin' over the recent past, I guess.'

George, seated directly opposite, had suddenly gone distant. As if some skeleton in his own cupboard had just been rattled. Wil wondered if he was offended by the request for time off, after so short a time in the firm's employ. Masters bent over, his brows drawn down, as if he had twinges from his hip.

Wil made one or two other light remarks and received no reply. Masters appeared to be breathing more deeply.

'Is anything wrong, George? Did I say something—'

With an effort, Masters hauled himself back to the present and his companion. 'No, it wasn't anything to do with you, Wil. I mentioned a weddin' an' reminded myself of something which had gone into the back of my mind. Maybe it's what has been troublin' me all day. A weddin' in South Loop City. One I really ought to be attendin'. An' yet I can't bring myself to go along there an' see the boss getting spliced. It's not like me, either. Can't help showin' a special interest, though, in the circumstances. What was it you said, you needed to take a day or two off to get your thoughts straightened out?

'Tell you what I'll do. I'll fill in for you, personally. Tomorrow, first thing. I'll ride for Clearwater an' stand in for you. How'll that be? The finest possible excuse for not goin' along to South Loop to attend the boss' weddin'. You'll be doin' me a favour, especially as the wedding is this weekend.'

'Whatever you say, George. You'll find it all straight an' above board. Me, I'll be glad of the short break, an' I won't stay away too long, you can be assured of that!'

Wil was relieved that he had not accidentally offended his normally genial boss. He poured generously for his host, lit a cigar for him and eased back in his padded seat to ask a few questions, as the opportunities presented themselves.

Five minutes later, he asked the big one.

'George, I feel I ought to have known a long time ago who it is that owns all the South-Western Traders stores. But I don't, you know.'

Masters pointed at him with his cigar. 'Well, don't feel bad about it, Wil. The boss is Charlie. Charlie Johnson. As a *permanent* manager you sure as hell ought to know that. Charlie Johnson, the one who is gettin' married in South Loop, later in the week.'

Wil nodded. 'What sort of a fellow is he? Younger than I am, perhaps? Must have a lot of go in him.'

For the first time since they met, Masters shook with mirth.

'Yer, I'd say about five years younger than you are, Wil. Sort of a will o' the wisp, if you know what that means. Given to travelling, on business. Sometimes as far as the west coast. On occasion, even further. It ain't no use you wrinklin' your brow, 'cause you only have to see Charlie once to remember forever.

'All that long fine auburn hair, dead straight an' over the shoulders. An' those flashin' green eyes an' that trim figure! Above all, Charlie has spirit. Still, it ain't no use keepin' you in suspense. It's clear you've been away from these parts for quite a while. Charlie is Charlie Johnson. Charlie bein' short for the proper Christian name, Charleen, Charleen Johnson. Does that mean anything to you?'

Wil stared at his companion, not giving any indication about the stunned shock he was feeling. He felt like a man in a prize-fight, who knew he was going to be knocked out the moment the blow was struck. And the blow was only a split second away in time.

Could George mean *that* Charleen? The one who had been a ward of his father? He listened intently.

'Charleen Johnson Mayer is her full name. Her Pa was a full-time sea captain, you ought to know. Away from these parts for most of the time. Charleen was put ashore some years ago, under the protectorship—if that's the right title—of one Henry Bollard, formerly a rancher in the South Loop region.

'Folks in these parts never knew Charlie's mother. Rumour had it she sailed with her husband and contracted a fever abroad, which terminated her life a trifle early. Eventually, Captain Clinton Mayer had to come ashore on account of wounds received during the war. He was looked after, along with his daughter, in the Mayer House, South Loop City, by two spinster ladies who were sisters—Miriam and Lettie Rodwall. The Rodwalls are still there, and Charlie of course uses the house as her home, when she's still in town. Which ain't often.'

George paused for breath, while Wil gulped his drink.

Wil spoke first, after the silence. 'How come this young woman ramrods all the stores in the chain, George?'

Masters ground out his cigar butt, and refused another.

'The Captain left the house to the sisters, an' his money to Charlie. As it happened, Charlie had a good business head, an' she knew the sort of business lines that would sell in these parts. One time, she went all the way to San Francisco to make contact with a sea captain plyin' between Calais, London and the west coast. Her Pa knew the man of old. That helped, of course. And she knew when to expand, when to take over a shop in another town, change its image and build it up. She's quite a woman, our Charlie.'

Masters nodded and winked, and gargled with his whisky.

'Who's she marryin'?' Wil asked, looking away.

'A good question, my friend. At one time, it was on the cards she'd marry one of the Bollard boys, sons of the rancher, you know. But although old Henry sent them away to get a good education, they didn't turn out to be the managing type of fellows. They were wild, stupid even, when they came back west to help out with their Pa's responsibilities.'

Wil continued to look away. He was wondering all the time what Masters would have thought if he had blurted out that he was Wilbur Coltman Bollard as soon as he arrived. The very notion brought him out in a cold perspiration.

'The older one came first, having finished his studies at about eighteen or so. He didn't really take to ranching. Not even to managing a ranch. There was trouble with the hands, a herd goin' north to be sold was decimated by rustlers. The older son was blamed. After that, he took off now and again. A drinker an' a gambler, he was. An' the two don't mix.' Masters yawned. 'A sad story, you'll allow. And the younger boy was just as shifty.

'I'd say it was due to their Ma not havin' settled in the west. She came for a while, looked around, then went back east. She looked after her boys when they went to Philadelphia for education, but she never came back this way. Not even when old Hank died.'

Wil's voice had altered when he repeated his question.

'Guess I've drunk too much, Wil. Let me see. There was some sort of a gents' agreement between Clinton Mayer, Henry Bollard an' Cyrus Grunbaum, who owns the South Loop section of the railroad. If Charlie didn't marry one of the Bollard boys by the time she was twenty-three, then she would be expected to marry one of the Grunbaum lads. In this case, the second son, Nathan. Known locally as Nate B. His older brother, Homer, appears to be permanently out of town, an' Nate has a wild streak accordin' to the rumours, which occur quite regularly.

'Ain't never a week passes but Nate is away in that luxury private railway carriage his Pa had specially made. He's up the line, through an' past North Junction, or down through the other way, headed for El Paso or somesuch place. Locations you an' me scarcely dream about. Wil, I can't tell if you've changed the mixin' of my drink, or if it's simply nature tellin' me I've had far too much.'

Wil gave assurances about the drink mix. 'So, Charlie has had her twenty-third birthday an' she's marrying that Nate fellow, later in the week?'

George nodded, and answered several more questions before confirming that the earlier arrangements still stood, and that he would be riding for Clearwater, early the following day.

Wilbur left him with mixed feelings. He had heard his own sorry past described, how his family had deteriorated and come to nothing, and how Charleen, his brother Richard's sweetheart, was going to marry one of the Grunbaums.

The older generation of Bollards and Grunbaums and Mayers might have respected and trusted one another, but there was no love lost between the offspring of the former two families.

Although he had worked hard over the previous ten or twelve weeks, Wil discovered that he had more energy than he imagined he possessed. Anger, deep and smouldering, ever since George Masters' revelations about Charlie and the Grunbaum wedding, had kept him pepped up with a great restlessness.

Since his siesta-time meeting with the general manager, he had paced the perimeter of the town, paced a room at the hotel, and paced along the long bar in the Creek Saloon. Even a long shower under a water-pump had not served to slow him down.

He resented his own past rearing up at him. He resented his younger brother's abysmal record, and he resented the way in which the Grunbaums were lording it as the most prestigious family west of the county seat. In the matter of the intended marriage, the Bollards were sure as hell having their noses rubbed in the dirt. Richard, apparently, had not been around his old local haunts for the best part of a year. And with old Henry in his grave, Wil was the only one in a position to suffer.

Charlie had been Rich's girlfriend; never Wil's. He had admired her, and she had been friendly towards him, but that was all. So, if Wil felt as strongly as he appeared to do about the coming event, it had to be family pride that was stirring him up. Walking with his hands on his hips, he banged a man's arm as the latter was raising his glass to drink.

In the old days he would have backed off graciously, but now he gave only a very casual nodded acknowledgement that he was in the wrong. A minute later, he chewed down hard on yet another small cigar and ruined it. He was burning himself up with passion, and he knew it. What could he do before he came to a decision about other, more weighty matters?

The drinking of whisky that afternoon with the manager had not appeared to do him any harm. His old craving for the stuff had not been re-created. His frowning gaze took in the card-tables. How would it be if he made a brief return to another of his old pastimes? Perhaps a spot of gambling would calm him down, so that he could sleep in the hotel bed.

He ignored the rattle of the ball in the roulette wheel, gave his attention to the private games. Eight tables, all green-baized tops. Thirty men lolling, smoking, drinking, flicking the pasteboards, all intent—more or less—on besting one another in a game of chance.

He strolled up and down, big stetson pushed back, staring to one side and then to the other. Two of the men were only toying with the cards. Another set of four appeared to have differences. One of their number did not appear to have much knowledge of English the way north American whites spoke it. Wil paused before them.

'Somebody thinkin' of droppin' out?' he queried boldly, talking around his cigar.

The man with linguistic troubles stared him out, but another who had been complaining most loudly suddenly stood up and brushed past Wil, leaving him to take over. He was introduced to the new emigrant whose name was Schulz, and the four of them settled down to play. The money remained fairly evenly distributed over the first half-hour. Schulz had certainly brought with him a shrewd knowledge of how to play the basic gambling games. He read the game well, and had a good memory, too.

The itch to cut a few corners came to Wil after some three-quarters of an hour. He withstood it the first time, and played on, not trying too hard. At the same time, the atmosphere changed. His luck was in, and as one fortunate move followed another his brows climbed his head a little further and stayed at an optimistic level.

Schulz, by contrast, began to perspire along the receding line of his dark hair. He removed his hat altogether, and still his perspiration appeared, slowly negotiating the lines in his forehead, one by one, and piling up on his brows.

Wil pushed the whisky-bottle over. Schulz declined. A cigar was also refused. A little later, Schulz addressed his friend in guttural German. Schmidt, the one with a full jowl and grizzled chin, actually blushed under his bristles.

Wil watched the eye-glances between them. The fourth man did not appear to be interested.

'What's to do with him?'

Schmidt grinned, showing a lot of small black teeth. 'My friend, he says you are cheating.'

Wil favoured the accuser with a long hard look. 'What do you think, Schmidt?'

The plump man fumbled with his cards, distributing black-toothed grins all round. 'Me, I am not sure.'

Wil's focus remained upon Schulz, who licked his upper lip, cleared his throat, and said one word: *'Cheating.'*

Enough was enough. Did a man tip over the table, which was quite light, or draw his revolver with lightning speed? Or what? If he had doubts about gun drawing, being out of practice, maybe he ought to try something else. He was mean enough to try and teach this newcomer a lesson, and reckless enough to use untried means. He grabbed the whisky-bottle with one finger left in it, pointed it at Schulz and aimed it at his head.

Many gasps went up from all sides, and the base of the bottle connected with Schulz's forehead, flew up at an angle and returned to the starting-point almost like a boomerang. Almost as a reflex action, Wil stuck up his hand and caught the neck of the bottle, lowering it heavily to the table so that the cards on it flew about in all directions.

He was as startled as anyone else, but he was not sufficiently reckless to attempt anything quite so bizarre a second time. Exaggerating his movement and his mood, he rose to his feet, banged the bottom of the bottle down on Schmidt's fingers and stared into his bloodshot eyes from two inches.

'I was *not* cheating, Schmidt! *You* ought to know that, you've been an American for longer than *he* has! I never cheat in the first hour's play! Comprende? And besides, you ought to teach him better words than the one he used. He's liable to get into trouble, an' you too!'

Schmidt started nodding, scarcely blinking. He was still nodding when Wil picked up a generous half of the notes and coins on the table and casually stuffed them into his pocket. With all eyes on him, he walked heavy-footed through the drinkers, and barged open the batwings with his spread elbows.

Outside on the sidewalk, it was at least cool.

His mind triggered off a repeat of the incidents at the card-table. His long-term anger turned to amusement when he thought of the whisky-bottle ricocheting off the tongue-tied Schulz's forehead and returning to his hand.

Maybe in the past he had taken his gambling too seriously, he decided. Maybe he had taken *life* too seriously.

Tomorrow he would make plans to thwart the Grunbaums, if his new-found determination did not go back on him.

One more job for that night: a trip to the livery to make sure George Masters took the shaft-horse and buckboard back to Clearwater. Come tomorrow, Wilbur Coltman Bollard aimed to become a saddle person again.

He belched gently without opening his lips.

FOUR

The following morning, Wil had a slightly dull head; not serious enough to worry about. He relaxed upon his bed with his eyes shaded from the sun for a while, and reread the letter from Uncle Clem before willing himself into action.

He ate a hearty breakfast, found that he still had sufficient resolution to look further into the arranged marriage between Charlie Mayer and Nate Grunbaum, and decided to do what he could to sabotage the event. Over breakfast, he came to the conclusion that the wedding would have to be postponed in some way. If he contrived a day or two more before the event, it would give him a chance to find out if Rich was in the vicinity and whether he still had a desire to marry Charlie.

Gossip which he had heard the previous evening could probably be turned to advantage. Hot Springs County was short on reverend gentlemen with fixed parishes. Consequently, many of the pious and religious folk of the region depended upon the services of two or three gentlemen of the cloth who moved around from one location to another, performing their functions wherever it was required of them.

In the southern part of the county, the parson best known was the Reverend Abraham Broadburn, a big, stocky, cylindrical fellow of some fifty-five years with a firm benevolent manner, a large appetite and a permanent blue-black chin. On this occasion, however, the Reverend Abe was said to be indisposed: laid up in his cabin with a lingering fever. It was fortunate for the widespread parishioners of the county that his cousin, visiting from Texas, was in a position to take over his duties for the period covering the wedding.

Due to their peculiar peripatetic duties, the clerics of the county had the use of several isolated cabins intended for overnight stays when away from home on duty.

In ordinary times, the Reverend Abe used to attempt to arrive in the town where he was to officiate at least one day before the event: two days, if at all possible. On account of Abe's illness, his cousin the Reverend Eli was behind schedule. As Wil rode determinedly from Newell in a south-westerly direction, headed for Bitter Creek, the Reverend Eli was almost certainly approaching the same town from Abraham's remote home on the eastward side.

Wil's aim was either to send Eli off in the wrong direction or in some other way to prevent his arriving in South Loop at the appropriate time for the big event.

By ten in the morning, Wil was more than half-way to his destination, but after that the high-stepping dun gelding which he had acquired began to tire and the rate of progress tailed off. Wil gave his mount a short rest, a brisk rub down and then forced it to work every bit as hard on the rest of the journey.

Around twenty minutes to noon, the rider had his first bit of luck. Coming in the opposite direction was Bitter Creek's hard-working medical man, a dour Scotsman with jutting sandy brows and a monster moustache. In between visits, Fred Bates wore a tam-o-shanter in place of his stiff black professional headgear.

On this occasion, he was in a hurry. He waved his tartan cap and shouted across to Wil, without attempting to stop.

'Good day to ye, laddie. If you have a minute when you reach town, look out for the reverend fellow. I hear tell he might want my services. Tell him to wait. I'll be back to deal with him presently. I've got to attend a delivery, you'll understand. I'm obliged to ye.'

Wil nodded and acknowledged, as

the gap between the sweating dun and the flying buckboard enlarged and was obscured by a cloud of dust.

In town, Wil asked three times about the arrival of the reverend. No one had seen him. He took time out to wash in a hotel, and seated himself on a verandah where he could watch the incoming traffic. Fifteen minutes passed before a man with a clerical collar came in from the east looking far from comfortable. Wil could have been the one to answer the newcomer's queries, but he wanted to observe him for a while before actually making contact.

Eli Broadburn was in his late forties, a tall lean man with a touch of the dandy about him. He looked like a man from the east, out of place in the west. Abe Broadburn was often referred to behind his back as 'Broadbeam' but this cousin with the lined forehead, short trimmed grey beard and big spectacles had little in common with his brawny cousin except for the dark suit and Quaker-style flat hat.

A little old Indian, unused to answering questions put to him by strangers, patiently pointed out the way to Mac Bates' surgery, and that was time for Wil to be on his way. He ran some of it, took a couple of short cuts and contrived to enter the surgery from the side entrance while the parson was impatiently knocking on the inner door, having entered from the front.

While Wil was recovering his breath, the caller cautiously opened the door a few inches and inserted his face.

'Ah, there you are, doctor, sorry if I disturbed you, but the fact is I'm due in South Loop very shortly and I need a bit of your professional help, first.'

Wil hesitated, but only for a few seconds. He nodded, smiled and indicated a chair, while he himself dropped carefully into Bates' swivel and toyed with a stethoscope.

'I'm overdue, out of town, where I have to make a delivery, sir, but I'll tarry long enough to advise you.'

Eli smiled behind his soft beard and moustache which were fine enough to be like those worn by venerable Chinese. 'The travelling, bouncing about all over the place on trails, I have to admit it affects my innards. Indigestion and the like. Leaves me feeling run down, just when I have a big wedding to attend to in the next town. And besides that, I have a fear of travelling alone any distance. I wondered if I could hire a guard, or two guards, capable men to escort me into the town of South Loop before the wedding? You seem like the person best fitted to advise me on such matters. What do you think?'

'I think I know what to do for the best,' Wil replied, warming to his pseudo-Scottish accent. 'You need a fairly long rest, medicine, and a couple of horse-riding guards. I'll see to it all. Firstly, a potion to take the discomfort out of the next mile or two. I'm sending you to a small cabin out of town. In fact, three miles nearer your destination. You'll have no trouble finding it. It's set aside for travelling gentlemen of the cloth, and there you'll rest.'

Wil stood up and went into Mac's dispensary, selecting a bottle of thickish white liquid which looked as if it had soothing intent, as well as being a sedative. He poured a generous measure into a small thick medicine glass and took it back to his patient, tipping some water into it and stirring briskly.

The Reverend Eli burped. 'How will I find this cabin, doctor?'

'Sign-posts, sir, indicating all the way, with an especially big one at the turn off. I'll visit you there, with a properly prescribed potion and the two guards. Right now, though, I'll have to leave you. When you get there, don't bother about grooming the horse, or anything. We'll see to that. You just rest.'

Wil patted him on the shoulder, ushered him out of the front door and watched him through the window. The pseudo-doctor's face was a mask of concentration. He was seriously considering the possibility of substituting for this unfit, scarcely known man of the cloth.

Apart from occasionally massaging his stomach, Broadburn looked to be holding up. He remounted his buckboard, called politely to the grey in the shafts, and turned the conveyance about. Unseen behind a lace curtain, Wil Coltman was pacing up and down the doctor's front hall, ignoring the possibility that Mac's housekeeper might return from the shops at any time.

Jake and Bluey Kimberley were brothers in their late thirties, tall, muscular and very sunburnt, on account of their being born in one of the hottest, driest parts of Australia. They each had a lot of dark sun-bleached hair, a bony forehead and a lantern jaw. In repose, they looked formidable, but, in fact, they were jovial sporting characters with a strong sense of humour.

A few years back, when the Circle B

Bollard ranch was a fine prosperous cattle outfit located to the west of Clearwater, and to the north of Bitter Creek and South Loop City, they spent most of their time in the smithy on the ranch.

When the spread was run down, and men were being paid off or sent away for their own good, the Kimberleys had not become bitter. Since they left their natal shores, they had known ups and downs in three countries, and they took their dismissal with a good grace. Due to their consummate skills, they soon found work in Bitter Creek. When work at the smithy dried up for a time, they hired out with Matt Cawthray, the saddler, and there were men who preferred a Kimberley saddle to the celebrated Cawthray article, but the brothers did not trade upon their growing reputation.

When Wil was on the skids, there was an occasion when he had actually won a fair amount of money at the gaming tables. Seeing Jake and Bluey drinking beer, he made a point of paying them a week's salary apiece, and they had never forgotten the gesture.

One hour after the Reverend Eli had driven his conveyance westward out of town, Wil Coltman was headed after him on a fresh horse, flanked by the Kimberley brothers who had willingly undertaken to help him in his present endeavours.

Jake was actually the older of the two by two years, but few could tell him apart from his brother, so alike were they in appearance and in their mannerisms. As a gesture of friendship, Jake always wore a dun-coloured side-pinned Australian bush hat, while his brother, Bluey, wore a shapeless undented hat of corduroy cloth.

'Just so long as you ain't plannin' any real harm for the reverend, we can go along with almost anything, Wil,' Jake was saying assuringly.

'I'm not altogether sure of my plans yet, Jake,' Wil returned breathlessly, 'but it all has to do with Miss Charleen an' a weddin' with Nate Grunbaum as the groom. I don't believe she's keen to marry into the Grunbaum family. I don't want her to. But the Bollards are to some extent to blame. She was *Rich's* girl, as you know. If there's any chance for her to keep her freedom, or marry a better fellow, I'll be seein' what I can do.'

'So you're aimin' to keep the reverend away from the scene of the weddin' for as long as possible,' Bluey prompted.

'That is so, Blue. I want to keep Eli sedated and still in that cabin until after the time of the nuptials.'

Bluey whistled, and his big skewbald flattened its ears. By contrast, Jake's buckskin snorted briefly and tugged sideways at the reins. Wil's borrowed roan quarter horse plodded steadily on without showing any real concern.

'The poor guy is in a bad way, as you'll see, boys. I'll top him up with a large dose of stomach medicine laced with the sleeping draught.'

After a brief silence, during which they were all thinking, Jake asked another question. 'Back there in town, you must have posed as the doctor. We can recall you dressin' up an' actin' different parts over at the ranch. Er, would I be right in thinkin' you possibly aim to pose as a parson, as well?'

Bluey whistled again, but Wil nodded and chuckled. 'I'm thinkin' of givin' it a try. Of course, if anythin' should happen to go wrong, the Grunbaums would have me skinned alive.'

Half an hour later, the trio turned off a narrow track into the swale where the special cabin was located. Broadburn had released his grey from the shafts and then attended to his own needs. He was stretched out on the single bed with his outer clothing discarded and a glass of cordial to hand. As they knocked and moved indoors, he was murmuring to himself.

'If only I didn't have any more trail

journeying to do I'd be a happy man.'

Wil removed his hat and went into his act as a doctor.

'How was the delivery, doc?'

Having checked Eli's pulse, Wil was sounding his chest. His thoughts took a few seconds to get around to the purpose of the patient's question.

'Oh, fine, fine, reverend. A boy, due to be christened Ephraim. Weight about seven pounds, I'd say. Mother an' infant both doin' well. I can't find anything seriously wrong with you. You need rest. Take my medicine. Sleep through the night. Don't attempt to get up until an hour or so after sunrise tomorrow. I can telegraph South Loop an' tell the weddin' party what's happening.'

Eli was about to start uttering anxious queries, but Wil waved him into silence, and spoke out again. 'I have with me two old friends. Trusted friends, I might say. Jacob an' Ezekial. Christened with good Biblical names, eh? They'll act as your guards, stay with you, attend you on your journey until you are in sight of your destination. By then, we reckon you'll be pleased to dismiss them.'

Wil warmed the potion, stood over the parson until he had drunk it all, and kept talking until sleep gripped him. After that, he relaxed a little and moved out of doors on tiptoe, accompanied by his accomplices.

'I want him to leave here at, say, nine in the morning, but not tomorrow, the day after. That'll give me time to plan something worthwhile.'

'But if he awakens refreshed tomorrow and insists on getting on his way,' Bluey interposed, 'what then?'

'Try another dose of the medicine. If that fails, tell him the marriage has been postponed for twenty-four hours.'

Jake did not seem any more pleased than his brother, but they accepted their part of the plot and shook hands with Wil when he rode off.

FIVE

By taking one or two short cuts, Wil approached South Loop City in the best time he had ever achieved. Not much over two hours. It was seven o'clock in the evening as he manoeuvred the long-legged roan into the town by the least conspicuous route.

After loosening the saddle, he tethered the animal in the passage beside the peace office and slipped indoors when he was sure there was no one in the building who knew him.

The new constable, O'Dowds, was twenty years of age: a young Irishman who had travelled west alone, so as to avoid following in his father's footsteps as a patrolman in New York City police department. He was keen, conscientious too, and he thought at first that a request from a stranger for a specific reward notice was somewhat irregular, but his bearded visitor was persuasive.

'Bollard is the name. Be a good fellow an' take a quick look through this year's reward notices, will you? I have to be sure whether this Richard Bollard is in trouble, or not. It'll be worth a dollar if you do as I say.'

'Can I ask what your line of business is, mister?'

Wil chuckled. 'You shouldn't really. Look at it this way, if there's a reward there should be a fellow keen to collect it, eh?'

The young peace officer at once took him to be a bounty hunter, and he complied. While he was sorting through a drawer full of notices and pictures, Wil studied those on the walls. This particular part of his search proved negative. Constable O'Dowds was disappointed: not so the enquirer. Wil handed over the dollar, and left.

If Richard was not known for law breaking in the local peace office, it meant that Wil could make his enquiries without hitting trouble at the outset. Next, he visited the house of Brad and Pearl Murphy. These two had lived and worked on Circle B property for a number of years. Pearl had kept a house for Henry Bollard, and Bradford had been his first foreman. In fact, the Bollard fortunes continued on the up and up as long as Brad Murphy was in charge of the cattle and the cattle drives. It was when he had withdrawn from active ranching after breaking a leg that Bollard fortunes went into recession. They lived in a small board shack on the northern outskirts of town with a small garden at the back and a swinging divan in front, suspended from the ceiling of the gallery.

Pearl answered the front door and failed to recognise Wil, as he kept his face averted.

'Who is it, Pearl?' Brad called from within.

Wil leaned beyond the puzzled female, and called: 'Wil Bollard, Brad. This wife of yours sure is getting short-sighted.'

Wil put an arm round the woman, and half carried her indoors, while Brad limped across the hall in his slippers to make him welcome. Brad's hair had receded since he left the spread and his waist had thickened considerably, but he still looked a formidable fellow on account of his lush brown moustache. Pearl, by contrast, seemed to have lost weight. White streaks in her black hair made her look more than her thirty-eight years.

Wil realised as they ushered him into an armchair that Pearl was peering as if she needed spectacles to see properly.

Pearl remarked: 'He looked well. He's filled out a bit, too.'

'And his hands are steady,' Brad added. 'He's kicked that drinkin' habit, thank goodness. It's great to see you, Wil, but what brought you into town this time, without any warnin'?'

'I heard tell of a weddin' which affected Bollard interests, Brad. Thought you might be able to bring me up to date about what's been happenin' in town. I wanted to ask you about Rich, and Charleen, and Nate Grunbaum. You'll think I've left showing an interest a bit on the late side, but I'm here anyhow, and I sure would like to hear a few details, even if they sound depressing. For the present, I'd like you to act as if you haven't seen me. Don't ask me what I plan to do, because I'm not sure myself. Besides, there might be an outcry of sorts from the groom's folks.'

Wil took the armchair on offer, stretched out his legs and accepted a cigar from his host. Pearl brought him a glass of her home-made fruit wine. As soon as the pleasantries were over, Brad leaned forward in his seat, elbows on knees and brow furrowed.

'About your brother. As a matter of fact, we can't say much on that score, Wil, on account of he hasn't shown up for nearly a year. We hear rumours, you'll allow. He's bummin' a livin' somehow, but this far we don't think he's been in any real trouble.

'He keeps clear of South Loop, and none of his old associates in town have been seein' him. Especially have we noticed him stayin' away of late, on account of Charleen and the weddin' mapped out for her by the three old men, if you know what I mean. Maybe you ought to go an' talk to old Israel Proudfoot. I reckon he'd know more than we do, seein' as how he was runnin' his agency until quite recently.'

Wil sipped his drink, nodded and raised his brows interrogatively.

'Regardin' Charleen. Well, she hasn't changed all that much. Just as all fired busy as ever. One day she's around, shoppin' an such like, another day she's out of town. Sometimes she goes horseback ridin' an' other times she takes a buckboard.'

Pearl flitted in from her kitchen. 'She's been known to take a lift in a freighter before today, Wil, an' occasionally she'll use a stagecoach, if it's goin' in her direction.'

The woman smiled and withdrew. It was clear to Wil that she was warmly affectionate towards Charleen, even if the two of them were some little distance apart on account of money and privilege.

'Charleen's in town,' Brad resumed. 'All ready for the wedding, we suppose, except that she hasn't been around chattin' up the locals about it. However, all women take these things mighty seriously, an' Charleen had an unusual upbringing, havin' a sea-going father an' no mother around.'

Wil reached towards the open fireplace and knocked ash off his cigar. 'You don't need to make excuses for the Mayer girl, Brad. Not to me, of all people. She was always restless, always on the move. Sounds as if she hasn't changed a lot. I only hope that whatever happens tomorrow Charleen isn't disappointed.'

'That goes for me, too,' Pearl called out.

After a brief pause, Brad shrugged his shoulders. 'What can I say about young Nathan Grunbaum, to you who knew him well? He's wild, dissolute, self-seeking. Given to mad schemes, like horse racin' an' rearin' horses to win future races. He'll gamble on anything, anything at all! Mostly, when he's in town, he's cookin' up some scheme or another for goin' up or down the line in that special private railway coach that belongs to his Pa.

'Sometimes, I think Cy gets sickened of him, only he won't crack the whip an' bring him to heel. Maybe that's because Homer, the older son, doesn't come around any more.'

Wil nodded. 'I had a letter from Uncle Clem, in Philadelphia. He said Homer was in prison for embezzlement, so maybe he'll be away for some time. Tell me, do you reckon Nate has any affection for Charlie?'

'He dances with her if there's a barn dance, but if one of his sidekicks turns up on a flash new gelding he's just as likely to go off on that an' leave Charleen to her own devices. She's game enough to take a turn round the floor with other fellows, but you can see she's doing it simply out of politeness. One thing Nate will find out. If an' when she's married to him, he won't hogtie her.

'Whatever it is takes her out of town so often, her business instinct if that's what it is, Charleen will not give up doing what she wants to do. I can't see her goin' off all the time on that fancy rail-coach, not unless she has some special reason for travellin' up the line!'

Pearl came in and quietly sat down between them, on a stool.

She sniffed. 'Arranged marriages might be all right for poor girls, but Charleen ain't in that category. She's got money, brains an' style. I don't believe any good will come of this marriage from her point of view. However it works out, Nathan won't be affected. His Pa will gloss it over if it turns sour. But the girl will be affected, you mark my words.'

Wilbur agreed with her. He allowed his friends to talk easily, and accepted a large helping of fruit pie before he insisted on leaving to search out more information before the town settled down for the night.

'One last thing, you two. If you see me around tomorrow, an' I've changed my appearance, it'll be best to ignore me. Pretend we haven't met tonight. Is that understood?'

Brad and Pearl both gave him their assurances. They also offered him a bed for the night, if he was without a roof over his head when he had finished his enquiries.

Israel Proudfoot. Owner of Proudfoot and Company, property agents, of Main Street, South Loop City. Proudfoot was one of the most flamboyant characters in a western town noted for eccentrics.

He was tall, bulky and overpowering as a personality. A mane of wavy white hair and a beard and moustache of large proportions featured on a nicely shaped head with a large hat-size. Mostly he was seen about town in a grey waistcoat and a dark suit. The painted notices over his double-fronted establishment informed the general public that he was an enquiry agent as well as a dealer in property. In fact, people interested him much more than timber and brick dwellings.

He smoked a meerschaum pipe and played vaudeville tunes on a small upright piano. Wil could tell as soon as he approached the building that Proudfoot was in his apartment because of the tinkling notes of the pianoforte coming from the upper storey.

Proudfoot had partaken of his extensive evening meal by eight o'clock and was entertaining himself (and some of his neighbours) by his nightly piano melodies which floated out through the open upper windows. Wil mounted the outer staircase at the end of the building and tugged at the bell-rope. Nothing happened within to break the sounds of music, but the visitor—knowing the eccentric resident's habits—patiently waited, and was rewarded.

Proudfoot came to the door, opened it, beamed and allowed his pince-nez to fall to the limit of their holding cord.

'Good evening, young sir. Do come in. It isn't often I have the pleasure of visitors at this hour. Do take a seat. Make yourself comfortable.'

In the slightly over-furnished salon with its lush drapes and glass-fronted cabinets there was a cloud of tobacco smoke put up by the pipe, lying on its side on top of the piano, positioned near a rear window.

Wil left his hat on the stand near the entrance door, slipped into an armchair and brought his hands together as in an act of prayer. Already he was practising for a part mulling over in the back of his mind.

'I'm making enquiries about a young man who used to spend a lot of time in these parts. His family is interested and so, no doubt, is Miss Charleen Mayer at this particular juncture.'

Proudfoot reseated himself at the piano, put the stem of the pipe in his mouth, but kept his full attention on his visitor. If he knew who he had admitted, he never mentioned it.

'I refer to Mr Richard Bollard, by the way. I've been informed that you once gleaned information in a professional fashion.'

Proudfoot cleared his throat. 'I see. If it's a friendly enquiry I don't mind telling you what I know, although more recently there hasn't been much.'

'Richard Bollard. Well educated. Restless. Unable to settle down. Tried cow handling, very briefly. Like certain others in these parts, he looked for excuses to move around. Liked to upset the more staid and prosperous members of our society.'

Wil began to colour up. Proudfoot noticed it, and went on, giving details for a change.

'On several occasions he has been known to harass passengers taking a ride on the trains which come through South Loop. Especially folks travelling on the private Grunbaum carriages. Windows have been shattered. On occasion, a man has flagged down the loco between towns and then merely asked the engineer what the time of day is.

'There have also been small anti-social acts against the Grunbaum household in town. All thought to be down to the high-jinx of the younger Bollard. Other times, the sheep herders who occupy the old Circle B ranching territory have complained about men harassing their flocks. Spirited dogs with their tails tied together have been sent in among the woolly creatures to cause a miniature stampede. Such acts are always likely to incense the owners of flocks of domestic animals.'

Wil cleared his throat, and replied. 'But it's a known fact that ranchers and cowhands, all sorts of people who have been involved with cattle resent the arrival of sheep, which they consider an intrusion. Are you *sure* Rich Bollard was involved in stupid tricks like that?'

Proudfoot talked round his pipe. 'Not altogether certain, my dear sir, but others in the town are. You'll allow the Bollards, dispossessed of their lands, are likely to have stronger feelings against the sheep men than ordinary cattle-inclined troublemakers!'

Wil merely grunted. 'There are other families in town with records for wildness as notorious as the Bollards, Mr Proudfoot. An' sons who don't come back to the family home any more might very well have the soundest of reasons for staying away.'

Proudfoot assessed that pronouncement for himself, and summed it up without asking for clarification. He smiled. 'Rich has not been around here for nearly three months. No one expects him. It is rumoured he's establishin' a wild life-style in townships on the main railroad route. And that's all I can tell you. I surely hope he doesn't start to run with the villains who occasionally hold up the trains and brandish pistols at the passengers. Clearly Rich has a grudge against society, but I'd better not go on.'

For a man of his bulk, Proudfoot moved swiftly. He stood up moved across to the door where Wil had entered and paused for his visitor to follow. On the way across the lush carpet, the visitor side-stepped a big sphere which was, in effect, a globe. It had upon it a great many medieval devices, in addition to the continents of the world and the sort of squiggles and symbols beloved of astrologers. Proudfoot blinked as Wil manoeuvred around the sphere, and smiled to himself.

'I have two passions to occupy my time, young man. You would probably guess that music is one of them. The other is astrology. Tomorrow's indications augur rather unusually for two people likely to feature in much publicised local events.

'One will live through a day most critical in her life, and the other has the most clear indications possible concerning deviousness, duplicity and double-dealing. I hope your readings for the morrow will be favourable. Good day to you, sir. I hope our meeting has been fruitful for you.'

Within seconds, Wil was out on the top of the exterior staircase and the door was closed behind him. The piano was back in action before he had started down the steps. The meeting with Proudfoot had certainly been of great interest. He found himself wondering if the old man really knew who he was, and whether the casually mentioned predictions really would occur in the way his host had suggested.

It never occurred to Wil that Proudfoot could have been speaking of anyone other than Charleen and Nathan. He stumbled down to street level like one in a daze.

SIX

Although the sapping heat of the day had long since passed, Wil felt as if he was being drained as he staggered away from the Proudfoot building. Over a pot of beer in a second-class saloon which was short on customers, he reflected that it was after nine o'clock at night: that the westering sun was almost down and that the shadows were deepening and shrouding the town at the end of yet another day.

He marvelled at the amount of effort he had contrived to put into his day since he rose at a comparatively early hour and rode like a pony express rider from Newell to Bitter Creek. The business at Mac Bates' surgery. The later secondary meeting with the Reverend Eli Broadburn in the parsons' retreat, west of Bitter Creek. Dealings with the Kimberleys, standing guard over the stand-in priest, and then another punishing ride into South Loop City where so many of his former associates lived.

Talks with a constable, with the Murphys, and—more recently—the short interview with Israel Proudfoot. And yet for a man contemplating *his* sort of intrigue, there was still much to do. Tomorrow was the stipulated wedding-day: the day of the ceremony. 'Let no man put asunder' and all that.

More contacts had to be made. Where should he start? His stomach gurgled with emptiness, in spite of the fruit pie which Pearl Murphy had forced upon him. A meal would have to wait. Now, he had to seek out a potential ally. He worked his way to the west end of the town, and turned south along a block of wooden houses off the ordinary grid of development.

Marta Hickstead, probably the oldest woman in town, lived in the fourth cabin. A permanent plume of woodsmoke topped her stove. She was never short of warmth, and her rocking chair was occupied nearly always, except for bunk-time.

As Wil approached, she called: 'Who's there? Don't be afraid to make yourself known; we don't have strangers in this here two-horse town! You're a stranger, iffen you don't know that!'

Wil grinned in the gathering gloom. 'Hold your horses, Marta, I'll be right with you.'

She had her wicker rocking chair out on the stoop and she wanted someone to help her get it back indoors. Her visitor waited until he was mounting the shallow steps to join her before he enlightened her further.

'Wil Bollard. I've had a long busy day, started in Newell if you'll believe me, an' there's folks in this town I don't want to know about my presence. So will you keep this visit to yourself?'

Marta was almost blind. Wil gave her a hug and helped her back indoors and then returned for the chair and a piece of knitting she had been working on earlier. She admonished him for being away too long, grumbled about this and that, but never criticised him for his irresponsibility, his wantonness or any other human failing which other townsfolk gossiped about.

They drank coffee together, and he shared a plateful of her stew, which was part of her staple diet, and they talked of this and that, confining all the gossip to a few years back.

'I want to borrow some of your dressing-up clothes, Marta. For a day or two. Maybe longer. I'll leave you a few dollars in the usual place, on the shelf. Do I have your permission to root around a little in Sebastian's old chest?'

'You surely do, old friend. And be sure to get rid of the moths, if you find any in there. Me, I think I'll make myself ready for the bunk. I'm sure you won't take it a miss. My old bones get to shake round about sundown these days. I always know when it's time to make my move.'

Wil put her at ease, and moved into another part of the shack screened by a long curtain and walled by a light partition. There, he found the big travelling leather trunks which he had come about.

Marta had not had a particularly easy life. Her husband, Samuel, was a repairer of watches and clocks, and other items with delicate mechanisms. His eyesight had gradually deteriorated, so that he had to do most of his work out on the verandah in sunlight. They had one son who, like many other sons of the west, was restless. Not for him the draw of the frontier. Sebastian, from the earliest age, was fascinated by grease paint. He wanted to be an actor.

So as not to cramp his style, they had allowed him to go off with some travelling players at the early age of fourteen. He had stayed away, playing the boards of the United States of America from coast to coast. He sent many cards and short letters, but his visits back home were infrequent.

The Civil War put him out of business. He returned to the old homestead then, but joined the army within a few weeks when local sons of his own age signed on. In the last six months of the war, Sebastian died in action. As if that was not sufficient grief for Marta, her husband died within a year. Ordinary heart failure, the doctor said, Samuel not being of a strong constitution.

And so the old woman was left alone. But not even her failing eyesight subdued her ebullient spirits. She had more friends in South Loop City than anyone else, and the confidences she kept to herself were far in excess of the special titbits which Israel Proudfoot sorted out for profit.

She was muttering, on this occasion. 'I'm goin' to get me a reader. Somebody with a pleasant voice like my Sebastian had. And somebody with patience. And I'm going to have 'em read classical books, like that Will Shakespeare wrote in plays—'

Wil answered in monosyllables and made vague promises, with his hands busy all the while with Sebastian's wardrobe. He found a grey jacket and trousers, plus a flat hat which was a remarkably good fit. Trying on the dog-collar and the black cloth which hung from it gave him food for thought. It was as if Sebastian's cold hand had him by the throat.

Plenty of old spectacles, with frames of different sizes and shape. The find which gave him the most uplift, however, was a wide bulky white cassock with a cowl. He felt that when he was under the scrutiny of the involved families in the church his ordinary disguise might be penetrated. But with the cowl and the spectacles, maybe he could bluff his way through the ceremony.

He hoped so, anyway. From her bunk bed, Marta called out a question. Her tone of voice suggested that she was almost asleep.

'What you dressin' up as, Wil?'

'It's a secret, Marta. But I have a question to ask you. Supposin'—just supposin' the priest takin' a weddin' service wasn't a proper priest. Not properly ordained, you understand. Would that mean the couple were married, or would there be no marriage at all?'

Marta was slow to answer. He thought she was asleep. He was about to slip away when she chuckled. 'If the priest wasn't ordained, the couple would still be single, after the event. That could cause a whole heap of trouble. Unless—unless one or more of the parties involved didn't really want a marriage to take place. What a funny notion to fall asleep on. Kiss me goodnight, an' be about your business, Wil. I hope the spirit of Sebastian is there to help you.'

Wil tucked her in, made sure that the stove was burning efficiently, and slipped away into the night. Like a wraith, he moved off in the white cassock, carrying duplicated clothing over his arm. Some of South Loop's more distant sounds began to carry to him. The time was nearer ten than nine. His eyelids were beginning to feel heavy.

The wooden church was a strong edifice with no ceiling, and a lot of overhead crossbeams in evidence. He lighted a single lamp near the pulpit, opened up a prayer book and another slim volume with the lines of the marriage service in it.

He had a feeling that there was a bat, or a trapped bird, hovering about somewhere, but the building itself seemed friendly enough.

The older Grunbaums, Cyrus and his wife Kate, their youngest son, Virgil, home from college, and their married daughter Sally from the west coast were all easy to locate, inasmuch as they were taking their ease on the broad gallery which fronted their house on Second Avenue.

A lamp lighted at each end reflected the smartness of the paintwork on the outside furniture and the jewellery on the ladies' dresses and hands. Virgil spotted Wil's approach before any of the others because the white cassocked figure came into his line of vision.

'Hey, Pa, here's the missin' priest. Now you'll be able to put your mind at rest about tomorrow!'

For his pains, Virgil was ordered by his mother to keep in his seat and refrain from making a fuss. Wil came up slowly. He introduced himself to Cyrus, giving the name of Eli Broadburn, and allowed the assembled company to assume that his health was slightly below par on account of rail travel. Cy wanted to press him to a glass or two of wine, but Wil argued against such a development, using as an excuse the fact that he had other calls to make.

Finally, he remarked: 'I suppose I ought to have spoken to your son, Nathan, sir, but if he's otherwise engaged at this time, tomorrow will do quite adequately.'

Clearly, old Cyrus, bulky, afflicted with an arthritic hip, and over-dressed, was embarrassed. His condition was in no way alleviated when one of his paid hands came up with a torch in his hands, and an excited announcement to make.

'All the lamps around the circuit are now lighted, Mr Grunbaum. And the competitors are at the start line. As you are already busy, Nate says for you not to trouble to go along and start the race off. So, if that's all right with you, I'll back off an' watch the developments.'

Cy waved him away. To Wil, he said: 'You see how it is, padre, youthful high spirits. My son an' his friends are determined to have a horse-race around the town, this bein' his last evenin' of freedom. Not in the best of taste, maybe, but only youthful high spirits, you'll allow.'

Wil murmured placating remarks, and

withdrew, walking with a stoop until he was rounding a corner. Unfortunately, he was still on the route of the horse-race. In fact, he had crossed it previously and was now quite close to the spot where it was to end. A crowd held him up. Accepting the inevitable, he straightened up, kept at the back and saw half a dozen mildly inebriated riders go by on sweating saddle-horses. Nathan was second, but the way he was riding and the expression on his full arrogant face made it seem very likely that he would become the winner.

There was a short period of suspense before a great outcry from around an intersection confirmed what everyone believed. Nathan had won. Men who had been in the street since before the race began surged into the bars knowing that free drinks would be set up for them.

A few others who had been buying in early, danced about on the sidewalks and made contests out of beer-drinking. Wil began to slide away. At the last minute, one of the men on the sidewalk came after him with a brimming beer-glass.

'Hey, reverend, drink this, why don't you? The hombre you'll be marryin' tomorrow has just shown he's the finest catch in town by winning a horse-race!'

Wil smiled. In character he replied: 'Being married is no sort of a horse-race, my son.'

He side-stepped the insistent reveller and managed to work his way round the first corner, but the beer-drinker followed him, his tone of voice changing. 'Reverend, I insist. And don't tell me your cloth won't allow you, 'cause *I* know different, see! *All* parsons can drink. I've known a lot of them myself. So here y'are. Drink it down an' I'll take the glass back. Nate will be pleased!'

Under his excess of disguise Wil boiled up. His temper was too far gone at that hour of the evening to stay in check. He drew away to measure his tormentor, drew back his right fist and slammed the other straight in the jaw. The drinker slipped backwards and measured his length in the dirt. His hat came off, his eyes struggled to focus for a few seconds and then he was away: unconscious for at least a couple of minutes.

Wil strode away. He muttered: *'Nate will be pleased,'* and spat on the ground.

He still was not quite clear where all his enquiries had brought him, but he plodded on once more, determined to go to his bed having done everything possible in the way of preparation for an all-out attempt to thwart the Grunbaums the following day.

The spinster sisters, Miriam and Lettie Rodwall, were an interesting couple. Neither of them had experienced anything other than being in service and similar work, but they were efficient and they made every effort to see their work well done.

Lettie was the older, at forty-five. She differed from her sister in temperament, having a Roman nose and an aggressive way of communicating. Miriam was milder, self-effacing almost in her gentleness: until some belligerent fool pushed her too far, and then she would show the real strength of her character. She, it was, who would bring out the shotgun and hold it in such a fashion that an inebriated bullying masher, or a lodger who had forgotten his manners, would know that she knew how to use it.

On the occasion of Wilbur's late-night visit, they had delayed the evening meal out of respect for Charleen and the Grunbaums and the impending wedding. Moreover, they had put on a few extras to the ordinary menu which had caused their food bill outgoings to mount up quite a bit. Lettie had figured they were seven dollars and twenty cents overspent for the week.

Wil refused to go into the parlour and take food with the regular lodgers. Instead, he seated himself in the kitchen-cum-servery, away from the warm stove and addressed himself to the toiling ladies as they alternated in delivering food to the festive table.

He learned that Charleen had been incapacitated with a slight headache and that she had retired to her bed early. Miriam noticed that he had grazed his knuckles on the right hand, and she insisted in taking time out to bathe the hand and strap on it a light bandage. She would most likely have been horrified if she had known the truth about how the 'wound' had been acquired.

Wil, out of sheer need, ate some turkey and bread and some special pie which Miriam had concocted from an old recipe.

After some twenty minutes, most of the food had been put through to the paying guests and the two women were able to linger in the kitchen and take a beverage, one which the priest also enjoyed.

In fact, Wil was feeling a lot of relief because these two sharp-witted women had not penetrated his disguise.

'Tell me, ladies, is the little woman

upstairs happy about her forthcoming marriage?'

The features of both women hardened. They exchanged conspiratorial glances. Wil perceived that they were against the wedding.

He said: 'Come, ladies, anything you tell me will be treated confidentially. Like it was told in a confessional, shall we say?'

Lettie remarked: 'She's not in a mood to discuss such matters. She has this wall of reserve. Always has had. Ever since her Pa died. It's hard to tell. The wedding is all to do with the three old men. Her Pa, Mr Henry Bollard an' old Cyrus Grunbaum.'

Lettie indulged in a deep breath, during which Miriam took over the explanation. 'In marryin' Nate she's honourin' some sort of a gents' agreement. Somehow linked with her twenty-third birthday. It could turn out all right, but we've known all the parties for a long time, and, well, in front of you, we can show our doubts.'

Lettie resumed: 'We understand that in some religions there are such things as arranged marriages. And that all parties to the marriage fully approve. However, my sister an' I, we don't approve of such arrangements. We don't think it's for the parents to say, or those standin' in for the parents. Other than that, we wouldn't want to say.'

Lettie beamed, showing formidable forked teeth, and signalling the end of the revelations. Miriam, the gentle sister, nodded and indicated that she had no wish to add anything further.

Well in character, Wil gave them an answer which pleased.

'Ladies, I am in full agreement with the views you have put to me. However, unless one or other of the parties to the marriage came to me and formally objected, I would have to go through with the proceedings. It would have been different if either party had been under age. And now, if you'll excuse me, I'll leave you. Excessive travel of late has taken its toll of me.'

He rose elegantly to his feet, gently shook hands with them and opened the back door. 'My regards to the young lady already in bed. I hope she'll benefit from a good night's sleep and be rid of her headache by daybreak.'

He stepped out into the street and stood quite still, for a minute or two: reflecting back to the time when Charleen shared the amenities of the Bollard household, when she had looked upon Henry Bollard as her guardian.

Had Charleen been happy then? Had the Bollards done her any good? Made her feel safe, secure? Or had they let her down: maybe passed on some of their own instability to her?

Would his actions on her wedding day improve her lot in life?

If he had not been so desperately tired, he could have thought the whole business through from the girl's point of view, and then maybe called off all his scheming for her benefit. All the action in the protracted day had left his mind stunned. He backtracked to the Murphys convinced he had to make his gesture at all costs.

SEVEN

Like a man sentenced to death, Wil awoke early and took himself off to a Chinese diner where he ate a hearty breakfast. In order to eat his food, he had to remove from his mouth the wads of cotton wool which he had put in there to make him appear fatter.

He was not attempting to look like Eli Broadburn. The real Eli was a man of different build: one which Wil was too heavy to copy. Consequently, all the latter was borrowing from the real parson was his name. It was fortunate that the Reverend Eli was a stand-in and not known by the staid citizens of South Loop.

Having eaten well and enjoyed his food, he left the diner and made his way to the church. A neatly dressed fellow in a dark suit with an Indian face was putting out hymn books and doing odd jobs. He made no attempt to talk, but he was wide awake: fully alive to what was about to happen.

Presently, a lean individual with a jerky walk slipped into the building. He was Spike Jensen, the pianist from one of the saloons. He took off his derby hat, left it in the vestry, and proceeded to dust off the piano before playing introductory music. Jensen could play almost any kind of music. However, on this occasion he played some traditional airs with a quite noticeable swing, and Wil came out from the back of the pulpit to have a quiet word in his ear before the congregation started to arrive. Spike took the admonishment well, and made the necessary adjustments in his style.

Wil felt fairly calm. He had read the marriage service through twice since he arrived that morning, and he felt that if he managed to get things under way without a mishap he would not make a fool of himself.

He paced, kept his head down and his cowl up. How he blessed the long-gone Sebastian Hickstead who had left the cassock among his valuables. Suddenly, a thought struck him. Who was going to give Charleen away? He felt sure the matter would have been taken care of, but for the life of him he could not think of a man associated with the girl who he felt was the likely candidate as a stand-in father. His pace grew heavier and his shoulders drooped a little. Thoughts about the father-substitute started him worrying in a rather depressed fashion about the shortcomings of the Bollards as a suitable family for a young woman bereft of parents.

A trickle of people, all neatly dressed for the event, slipped into church and began to occupy the seats near the back. Spike Jensen stiffened his back, and Wil passed to him a sheet of paper on which he had put down the numbers of the selected hymns in the hymn book. Spike's cheerfulness made Wil smile, in spite of everything.

He went back to his pulpit and there crouched over in an attitude of prayer.

Fifteen minutes later, the Grunbaum carriage drew up. Townsfolk who were not planning to enter the church made a crowd and gave them a cheer. Nathan's full face and sprouting narrow moustache looked as if they had been scrubbed and brushed. He had taken a glass or two of wine to settle his nerves. Fortunately, he was not prone to redness of the eyes which would have shown excessively in orbs as bulbous as his.

A fine stiff collar topped his starched shirt, but it pinched at the neck where he'd added a small amount of flesh in recent months. Cyrus led his small troupe down to the front of the church and occupied the appropriate pew.

Cyrus put his silk topper under the seat and eased his collar away from his neck. His wife, Kate, approved of her youngest son, her daughter and her son-in-law. Quite soon her eyes were surveying the forty people assembled, her head shifting this way and that in a bird-like motion.

The Indian had hung up the numbers of the hymns from a hook on a wall, near the piano. Eight youths who were the choir sidled in from the corner room at the opposite side to the pulpit. As they took their places behind the piano, four either side of the building, Wil began to feel that he was hemmed in. His mouth dried out, and he hoped against hope that he would be able to speak when the time came for him to commence his self-imposed ordeal.

The congregation had swelled almost to sixty when someone out-of-doors tapped significantly on a window, and Spike tailed off his overture music, straightened his back and launched himself into the wedding march, using plenty of loud pedal.

In order to get his mouth on the move again, Wil said over a prayer which he had learned at a very early age. He had finished reciting it before the bride and her party were half-way to the front.

Wil rose and flexed his muscles. His lips were still busy. Inadvertently, he was saying, *'Rich Bollard, where the hell are you at this vital time?'* Just when Wil felt that it was all too much for him, he recollected his earlier quandary about who was giving the bride-to-be away. Curiosity came to his rescue.

The man doing the honours was an obvious choice, really. He was tall, lean and weather-beaten. In order to accommodate Charleen he controlled his deep-sea roll with a fine muscular effort. Conrad Levoloski had sailed with the girl's father, Clint Mayer, as his first mate. He was a solitary, aloof type of person, utterly devoted to the late Clint, and therefore ideal to accommodate Charleen. When he was not managing the South Loop branch of South-Western Traders, exhibiting his admirable aplomb, the fifty-year-old former seafarer was exercising one of his many unusual talents. He spent time star-gazing from his apartment above the shop, and also designed garments in cloth and wool from styles seen in his travels. His neat, short brown hair had been clipped that very morning: so had his beard and moustache. The monocle gracing his left eye made him look like an aristocrat.

When all were seated, Wil did a few breathing exercises and went into the talking part of his act. He was able to throw his voice lower than normal, and he felt the pads in his cheeks further disguised it. He announced the reason for the congregation being there, and called upon them to sing the first hymn.

Half-way through, he noticed a bit of

agitation among the Grunbaums, but as it did not appear to be directed against him personally he paid little attention to it and concentrated upon retaining a calm outlook. The last verse had just begun when a late arrival hastened into church, paused at the back of the pews and tried to recover his breath. He was holding a grey derby hat, similar to that worn by the groom. He held it firmly in his two hands like a rugby player preparing to rush forward in an attempt to score a try.

Willie Bridson. The best man. Willie always seemed older than Nate inasmuch as his black hair had gone from forehead to crown. Otherwise, he was hirsute: it showed in his short black beard which linked his sideburns. He usually shaved his upper lip clean, but on this special day his collar, his jacket, his upper lip and other details suggested that he had arisen late, probably with a hangover from the stag night on the previous evening. His

Roman nose was bent, giving him the look of a prize fighter. On this occasion, his thin almost lipless mouth was open, assisting with his breathing.

The congregation turned in ever-increasing numbers to take a sly look at him. At last he plucked up courage to move forward, and he just made it in time to join the groom as Wil called the principals forward to begin the ceremony. Clearly, Willie had been the cause of the Grunbaums' nervousness.

Wil moved into position with a slow measured tread. His eyes were drawn to Charleen, although he fought to avoid paying too much obvious attention to her. She had a slight but shapely figure, faintly reminiscent of an hour-glass. Over her smooth kite-shaped face with the distinctive high cheek-bones a lightweight veil hung down from her tiny hat. Her full mobile mouth was still, but her restless green eyes missed nothing. Her long straight auburn hair had been brushed out without any fixing pins. It hung like a copper cowl to an inch lower than shoulder level. The shimmering white dress hugged her down to the ankles. Small skeletal high-heeled silver shoes, specially imported from Europe, raised her two inches higher than normal.

Conrad Levoloski acknowledged his duty of giving away the bride, and retired to his seat. Nathan, bulky and self-conscious, shuffled nervously with Charlie beside him. The sun's rays through the end window highlighted the thinning patch of hair, back from his forehead and accentuated the shadows under his full eyes. His luxuriant freckles darkened his fresh complexion and added colour to the big spatulate fingers on the hand holding Charlie's.

Wil intoned the set sentence from the service in the prayer book. He kept the slight panic out of his voice, and yet he was shaken when Charleen suddenly gasped. Through his masking glasses and her shading veil their eyes met, and Wil knew at once that she had recognised him. Had he been careless, or had she merely known through his familiar intonations who he was?

The text carried him through. At least, the girl was not panicking; nor was she seeking to delay or forestall the critical part of the service. Nate, so close to her, was busy with his own nerves and the unsettled condition left behind by his over-indulgences.

Charlie swayed, but showed no other sign of her shock. All went well until Willie Bridson had to produce the wedding ring. He stuck a blunt thumb in a waistcoat pocket and came up with an old curtain ring. Only the principals saw it, and yet they were all mildly shocked. Charleen coughed, and Nathan spoke words of admonishment out of the side of his mouth, warning Willie not to play the fool. Charleen's shoulders shook. Wil's lenses misted up a little. Jensen, the lean hollow-eyed piano player, slowly came to his feet in his best striped suit. He lifted the tumbler off the top of the carafe of water on the piano top, carefully poured until it was half full and then walked across to the principals with his slow jerky mode of travel.

Charleen took the glass with a graceful nod. Spike retreated. The bride lifted her veil and drank, and then handed the tumbler to Wil. Without thinking, he drank what was left in the glass while Charleen veiled up again.

Willie found the proper ring in the pocket on the other side of his waistcoat. He handed it over with a murmured apology, and accepted the empty tumbler at the same time. Nathan took the ring, and Wil resumed. His tongue rolled around their full names. Nathan Blackstone Grunbaum and Charleen Johnson Mayer. The last few critical utterances were achieved without incident, and Wil found himself concluding the service without being fully in touch.

Jensen's piano playing brought them back to reality with some stirring manipulations of the keyboard. The old Grunbaums lined up with the newly married couple. Willie Bridson mopped himself down, gasping with relief, and Nate took his cue from the silent Indian attendant who moved smoothly across to the door of the vestry and quietly opened it.

While the newly weds and their kinsfolk and attendants moved into the vestry, the congregation began to relax and chatter among themselves. As far as they were concerned, the wedding had been a great success.

One after another, the signatures went into the written record of the wedding. Cy Grunbaum pumped Wil's hand and was effusive in his thanks. He continued in that frame of mind until his wife, Kate, arrested his levity with a piercing glare from her beady eyes.

Charleen made a good job of kissing Kate's lean rouged cheeks, and returned

Nathan's early embrace with some show of warmth.

'You're still lookin' a bit pale, Charlie,' Nate remarked. 'Are you feelin' all right now?'

'Just a little bit under the weather, Nate, nothing for you to bother about,' she assured him. 'I won't be needing the doctor this trip.' The bride turned and gave Wil a frank smile. Her veil was no longer in use, but Wil still had his spectacles in place. She murmured: 'Thanks for everything, reverend. I hope your cousin Abraham will soon be better. And we'll see you along at the town hall very shortly, I hope.'

Wil answered in a low voice, confessed to being under par, but assured her that he would get in touch without delay.

Quite soon after that, the Grunbaum carriage pulled around to the side entrance, and those who had attended the signing began to leave and get into the vehicle. The crowd from the main entrance surged round to see them off, even though they were not going any distance. Charlie waved and blew kisses, while Nate waved his hat and went through the antics of a victorious sportsman.

Wil went back into the vestry and closed the door. He flopped into a chair and produced a cigar from under his vestments. Soon, he was drawing gently and wondering when and how he could relax more.

The town hall, which Cyrus liked to call the City Hall, was another huge barn-type building with a raised-up stage, and two tiny ante-rooms. Already, some thirty people had worked their way into the hall, and most of them were seated in chairs and benches which had been placed around the walls, leaving a lot of floor space for toing and froing and, ultimately, for dancing.

A trestle-table was in the middle, arranged lengthwise, with snow-white cloths on it and the big cake prominently displayed with a paste model of a locomotive decorating the top. Stacks of sandwiches and fruit and an array of pies covered most of the rest of the surface. Nearer the stage, a big silver container of punch vied with a barrel of beer on a table which was already stacked with dozens of glasses and tankards. Small wooden containers of wine were spaced out on a third trestle-table.

A few selected helpers distributed glasses for the toast, and others carried the carafes of red, white and pink wines. Willie Bridson called the hall to order, and the secondary part of the ceremony began. Conrad Levoloski spoke feelingly about Charleen's reputation as a business person, and the esteem which so many people in the county felt for her. He then thanked Mr Grunbaum for personally footing the bill for all expenses, and asked for a toast to the bride and groom.

This took place with decorum and was followed up by a noisy bout of spontaneous hand-clapping. After that, the cake was cut, and Charleen suggested that most of it should be cut into slices and handed out for as far as it would go. Kate Grunbaum didn't look too pleased at the suggestion, but she refrained from offering any observations.

Soon, the waiters were busy. Those who were most hungry queued up for food, while others lolled back and had their glasses refilled. A small four-piece band, consisting of Spike Jensen, a drummer, a guitarist and a violinist, moved up onto the stage and began to check up on their instruments.

Charleen and Nathan trod the floor in a waltz, and also started off the reel which followed. Some time later, Charleen asked Nathan to excuse her, and retired into one of the small ante-rooms which had been set aside for the bride and her two small maids.

Wil Coltman by that time had divested

himself of the warm white cassock. Thinned out to a dark suit, dog-collar and a quaker-style flat hat he felt almost like a different fellow. However, he retained his spectacles and the pads in his cheeks.

Presently, he found himself outside the window of the bride's retiring-room at the packed hall. The window was open to allow a passage of fresh air. He tapped on the pane hopefully. Inside, Charleen gasped and moved nearer.

'Who is it?' she gasped.

'It's me, Wil. Are we able to talk?'

'Hell an' tarnation, Wil Bollard, will you tell me what you are up to? I know you've been away for a while, but no one knew you'd been to a seminary for priests, nor that you would turn up using a false name!'

Wil kept his gaze away from the window. A couple of inebriated guests staggered by him. He coughed loudly to warn Charleen, who kept her lips sealed with a great effort.

Her voice sounded more determined than ever when she resumed.

'What can you tell me about a wedding performed by a man who is not a priest?'

Wil cleared his throat. 'I have to tell you it is *not* a proper wedding.'

Charlie's gasp turned into a long fluted whistle.

EIGHT

Somehow or another, Charlie's whistle—which he had known about since she was much smaller—brought Wil out in fresh perspiration. He found himself glancing up and down the street and imagining all kinds of calamities, like a whole crowd of important people finding out who he really was and the Grunbaums having him run out of town—or worse.

He backed away from the window, almost panicked enough to run away and then went back again when he saw a finger beckoning him closer.

'I've put you in a predicament, Charlie, an' I'll admit it. Things look black at the moment, but maybe we can work something out. Most of all, we've got to talk.'

'We're talkin' now, Wil Bollard, but nothing we say seems to have any special bearing on what's been done! What are we going to do? Admit to Cy an' Nate they've been duped, and then start over again? What do you have in mind?'

Wil coughed on smoke. 'What's it like inside? Do you think you could make an excuse for the two of us to have a private conversation, uninterrupted? After all, we're both intelligent people! We ought to be able to come up with something.'

Charleen shrugged aside her feeling of hopelessness and forced herself to think about practicalities. 'Well, the guests are all in the process of gettin' liquored up, at Cy's expense. Nate is in a good mood, at the moment. He approved of the punch, that means. I guess I could get my in-laws to permit a private conversation between the two of us. You'll be givin' me guidance, I suppose.'

Wil turned about and stared into the

pretty distracted face which confronted him. He was not sure whether Charleen was being sarcastic, or not.

'Give it a try. If they won't permit it, you'll have to come out on a pretext to some other place. Try for a meeting where you are now.'

The girl waved him into silence, partially closed the window and went away. Left on his own, Wil strolled a few paces in one direction and then returned. After what seemed an eternity, two men emerged from the hall entrance, stepped clear and looked up the street. Levoloski pointed. Wil studied his expression and learned little. Being an eastern European, Conrad was slow to smile and hardly ever laughed. Cy Grunbaum was more demonstrative. He waved his hand in Wil's direction and requested him to approach, making a grand gesture with his arm.

Wil discarded his defensive crouch, adjusted his flat hat and stepped jauntily towards the two older men. Cy aimed a large cigar at the cleric, and then handed it over.

'Say, padre, my new daughter-in-law requests a short private conversation with you. I hope you won't look amiss on such a request. Probably, she's just feelin' nervous, wants guidance. Very likely you're best man to give it, too. Come on in, an' by all means join in the festivities afterwards. As you know, we were expectin' you.'

Wil took two deep breaths. He allowed himself to be ushered through those guests who hover about entrances. With his hat doffed, he nodded his way through the queues and made an expression to show he approved of the music group. And then, he was through the door and in Charleen's presence. Alone.

She came and stood in front of him. Rather stiffly, he embraced her. She wilted a little and laid her head against his chest. He sighed, and kissed her on the forehead, not quite knowing whether he did so out of affection or still in the rôle of a marrying priest.

Her green eyes impaled him, almost. 'I suppose you realise, Wil, that in failin' to denounce you at once I am compoundin' what you have done. If compoundin' is the correct word. It makes me a part of your deception. Makes it into a conspiracy, the wicked work of at least two people.'

'I do realise that, Charlie. I'm pleased you ain't married to a Grunbaum, an' sorry I put you in a spot.'

By tacit consent, they held hands and walked further into the room, seating themselves on adjacent chairs, not far from the window. Charlie had by this time discarded her wedding gown and instead donned a light summer frock of green material. Wil took off his spectacles and regarded her quizzically.

'Why didn't you shout out when you recognised me, Charlie?'

'All along I had an inklin' you showin' up would mean I wasn't marryin' Nate.

And I believed I'd put you in a hell of a spot if I told what I knew. Before we get down to any plans. But *why* did you do it? Not just because you hate the Grunbaums, surely?'

'If I say I'm hazy on the exact answer, you'll find it hard to believe me, Charlie. Fact is, I had this notion you always belonged to the Bollards, seein' as how Pa was your guardian for a time. Then I got to thinkin' how I hadn't done the family name very much good in the last year or so. Stands to sense I'd let the family down. Then, I tried to pin down my thoughts to how it had been between you an' Rich. An' I believed I ought to interfere, make a gesture in favour of the Bollards. Something like that. Havin' been on the skids, what with gamblin', drinkin' an' such, I hadn't been in touch for quite a while. Hadn't seen South Loop City, hadn't seen Rich, an' hadn't seen you.

'When I heard that there was to be a weddin' with you as the bride, something happened to jog my memory as to how things used to be. And how you was supposed to marry a Bollard before your twenty-third birthday. I got to thinkin' that maybe you were bein' pressurised by the Grunbaums, now that the Bollards were a negative quantity. So, as you can see, I just didn't want you married into the Grunbaum family. And that's why I've done what I did. If I had time, I'd tell you that you're a whole lot more attractive than you used to be, an' although I'm scared stiff at times I'm glad I did it.'

Charlie tapped her foot nervously. Then she giggled, and reached over and squeezed Wil's knee. At length, she shrugged rather prettily and beamed at him. At that moment a shaft of sunlight shone through the thin copper curtain of her hair. Wil saw it and gasped.

'I don't have any strong feelin' for Nate. An' that goes for the rest of the family, too. I get this restless yearnin' to go places. Nate seems to have something of the sort when he's hightailin' it up an' down that section of railroad line his Pa owns. But me, I get it from my own father, a seafaring man. Maybe the Bollards have it, too. Maybe we're all products of the shiftin' frontier, of frontiersman blood, if you like.

'I've always supposed our three families were different, that I'd marry into one or the other. Nate was one of a group of people who grew up together. That's all. One of the gang, I suppose.

'Now, you an' I, we've got to face facts. If it comes out at present what's happened, you're for the bullet. I can really believe Cy, pressed by his iron-hard wife, might have you eliminated. Don't forget the old ties are weak now, since your Pa died. As for me, I can't allow that to happen.

'If I didn't protest, if I went through with the deception without revealin' what I know, Nate would possess me. Let's face it, it's what all men expect. I'd have to be in his bed tonight. Consummation of the marriage is the sober way of puttin' it. Knowin' I'm not really married to Nate makes it impossible for me to go through with it the way he wants it. But how can I avoid the obvious tonight?'

Wil's pulse was racing. 'Why don't you come away with me? I'll protect you. It's time for me to slip away into oblivion, anyway, because tomorrow the real priest will come riding into town and the balloon will go up. Even if it looks like a simple act of runnin' away, I think it would be the best thing to do, for both of us! What do you say?'

Breathlessly, he rose to his feet and crossed to the window, staring out at the false fronts across the dirt of the street while the muscles at the angles of his jaw rippled under his recently acquired beard.

'If you like we could ride to where Rich was last seen. Towards the county adjacent to this, on the westward side! What do you say, Charlie?'

Charlie rose like a mannequin, and

sidled up behind him. 'Let's not forget, Wil, there'll be lots of folks with a keen eye for the bride. We couldn't simply ride off in daylight, could we? That would ultimately brand us as conspirators, and then we'd be hunted. The Grunbaum pack would be out in force.'

She paused, leaning against him very gently.

'Besides, there's an alternative. If we look at things in the short term.'

Wil turned and gripped her lightly by the shoulders, looking into her clear green eyes with an intensity which surprised her.

'In short term? You mean as regards tonight. What is your alternative, Charlie?'

'We have to put off the groom!'

Wil gasped. He glanced over her provocative figure, blushed and then blinked several times. He could not imagine any young man he knew being put off from the first night of his wedding.

'You underestimate your own personality, Charlie. You could win a beauty contest in all the counties of New Mexico territory, an' that's no exaggeration. How on earth could a—er—healthy young animal like Nate be put off?'

'We'd have to dangle a very tempting proposition in front of his nose. Something that would attract him more than his first night with his bride. I'm surprised you can't think of anything, Wil.'

He grinned. 'I'm standin' too close to you to think of anything that requires a clear head, *amigo*. You'll have to spell it out for me.'

'Okay, then, *amigo*, hear this. Horses. In particular, race horses. He likes to back winners in races. Better than that, he would like to own racing stock. The kind of horses an' mares reared for speed. Well-bred quadrupeds, Wil. The sort which sire and dam racing stock of the future. I happen to know that he has his eye on a certain mare which is about to foal at any time. The property of a sharp-eyed breeding character who is domiciled in

North Junction. Luke Rottenberg for some reason doesn't like Cy Grunbaum. Moreover, Rottenberg has good friends with business interests on the main line of the railroad, the South-Western Pacific, and they think the Grunbaums are upstarts.'

'So do I, little Charlie, and all this conjecture about horses is very interesting, but I keep hearing the dancers and the boozers next door. Where is it leadin'?'

'When the mare, Cascade, produces her offspring he will either rear it himself, or sell it to a very high bidder. On account of the stallion. Geyser, having won several races before being put to stud. Rottenberg doesn't want his foal to go to the Grunbaums, although money talks with him.

'If Nate is to own the foal, he'll have to be there himself to ensure his bid is the highest, and he'll be up against a few well-heeled gentry who don't like takin' no for an answer.'

'So, we have to find out when Cascade is about to produce. Is that it?'

Wil's scowl revealed that he was absorbed in his partner's scheming deliberations. He was surprised when Charleen shook her head, brushing his face with perfumed tresses.

'Be realistic, Wil. We arrange for an urgent message to reach Nate. Coming by telegraph, supposedly from a friend close to Rottenberg. That ought to do the trick. What do you think?'

'It's a positive act,' Wil admitted, in spite of his own innate scepticism. 'I'll certainly go along with it, if you think it will do our cause any good at all. It ought to protect you, for tonight at the very least.'

As the full purport of his words were borne home to the pair of them, he grabbed Charleen to him and hugged her fiercely. She responded, and their lips were joined in a frantic kiss when someone tapped lightly on the door. The two of them were startled. Their lips came apart. Neither of them showed any feeling of guilt: only awareness. Wil put Charleen gently away from him, crossed to the door and called out to know who it was.

'Willie Bridson, padre. We wondered if the two of you were all right, an' whether we could get something for you to drink. Something restorative.'

The best man had spoken well; as Wil paused before answering, a loud burp came from beyond the door, destroying the feeling of tension which had suddenly built to a climax.

'We've nearly finished our deliberations, Willie. Bring me some whisky, if that's in order. And some wine for Mrs Grunbaum. She's still not quite at her best, I'm afraid. Oh, and if you have a paper pad and a pencil, I'd be obliged. I want to write something down for her.'

Willie burped again, stammered out a repeat of the order, and went away. Wil left the door and returned to Charleen, who examined his bearded jaw with some interest.

'You're not so fat, so dissipated as I thought, Wil. You've been swellin' your face with padding. Maybe you ought to have been an actor, after all.'

Wil was pleased. 'I had a liquor problem at one time, but that's behind me now. Say, how do you keep as slim as you are, Charlie? I seem to remember you used to have a very healthy appetite.'

'I still have, Wil, but I do ride a fair amount, and then I take exercises.'

Wil looked rather mystified, but he believed her when she gripped her hands together, stretched her arms above her head and gently arched her body, first to the left and then to the right. The return of Willie Bridson put an end to an interesting demonstration. Wil opened the door sufficiently to admit the drinks, and then they were alone again. Charleen toasted a promising actor, while Wil replied with a more telling one.

'To you, Charleen. May you avoid unnecessary entanglements, and marry the man of your choice. Only when the time is ripe.'

They clicked glasses, looked long and earnestly at each other, and reluctantly returned to the unfinished business which was troubling them. Eventually, they managed to concoct a message for a telegraph clerk. One which would draw Nathan Blackstone Grunbaum away from his unorthodox marriage in search of the ownership of a desirable quadruped.

It read:

Come in person at once for auction of foal everybody wants. To North Junction. Bring cash. Do not delay. Action early tomorrow. Flying Spray.

A friend.

Wil nodded over it several times. 'I'll see what I can do,' he promised.

'And I'll see what I can do about being

indisposed tonight,' Charleen added.

Wil thought she would have a hard job, if Nate got close enough to inspect her. She looked radiant, apart from her known pressing problems.

NINE

A priest with whisky on his breath in a town trying to make up its mind between extended free eating and drinking on the one hand, and a nice restful siesta on the other, could prove quite a problem to anyone who had the misfortune to get in his way.

Wil Coltman Bollard was both for and against siesta. On this occasion, his morale was boosted by special considerations and also by the best Scotch whisky available in town. He was using the hottest part of the afternoon to infiltrate that part of the town where the telegraph office was located without drawing a lot of attention to himself.

In fact, he achieved the office on Second Avenue south with the minimum enquiries as to his health and the state of the newly married couple. He found the office in question with the drapes pulled: as if the clerk in charge had taken it upon himself to go off to the wedding and make a day of it.

His hopes were sinking as he knocked on the door and counted off the seconds before there was any sort of reaction. His hand, bunched into a fist, was raised to knock a second time when the door opened a fraction and a homely face, located a good foot or so lower than anyone would have expected, peered up at him through extremely bright dark beady eyes.

'You picked a bad time to call, sir, and I don't think I'll be able to help you.'

Wil glared down at the black eyes and heavily thatched dark head in which they were embedded. 'If you open the door wide and ask me in, that could be a useful start,' he advised.

The dwarf, a mere five-feet nothing in height, patiently ran his fingers through his dark quiff, stroked his placid shirt over his bulking chest and then complied. Wil pushed open the door for the last few inches, and was met by a stale atmosphere sharpened by the smell of a recent curried meal.

'If it's business, reverend, I have to tell you that Slim Porter, the regular clerk, ain't in the building. Me, I'm his understudy, sometimes called Moose Malone.' The undersized character sprang up onto a high stool with a movement which showed the length and strength of his outsize arms. He began to chuckle. 'That's on account of my size, you understand. Then again, a lot of folks call me Bloke. I don't rightly know why, but I am not offended by such a nickname. So, if you feel like it, you can call me Bloke.'

'If that's the way you want it, Bloke it shall be,' Wil conceded. 'Now, can you tell me if Slim Porter has gone to the wedding? If not, where can I find him?'

Bloke mopped off his neck with a soiled

handkerchief. He appeared to have his scant brows permanently raised, his eyes were set so deeply under his bony forehead.

'At this time of day, Slim takes it easy. Not many messages come through during siesta. I can tell you for sure he didn't go to the weddin' reception. He don't like the Grunbaums. So much so, he won't even drink their free liquor.'

'Are you able to send and receive messages yourself?'

'Officially, the answer has to be no. I'm kind of heavy on the key, an' if anything goes wrong Slim could get in big trouble. So I wouldn't want to send anything while he's out.'

Wil took a couple of deep breaths, steadied himself, and resumed his questioning. 'Out where, then?'

Bloke grinned briefly, toyed with his nostrils and prepared to daydream. Wil disturbed him by getting off his stool and pacing dramatically across the worn floor.

'I—er—I don't rightly know—er—padre.

He drinks quite often with Mexican friends in one or other of their *cantinas,* but I don't know which one he will be in today.'

'How old are you, Bloke?'

'I believe I'm forty years of age, reverend. Not certain, but—'

'That's near enough,' Wil cut in brusquely. 'You're old enough to know the telegraph company rules don't permit any clerk to close up his premises during the hours of daylight and so lose business for the firm. Now, if Slim means anything to you, out you go an' find him. Get him back here with the minimum of delay, even if he is drunk! Is that understood?'

Bloke relaxed as Wil released the cloth of his shirt and jacket. Bloke went slowly to the door, opened it and walked slowly off in the direction of the Mexican area.

Wil gradually managed to calm himself. He felt that his stars, or whatever controlled his luck, had let him down. Charlie's fabulous notion for getting rid of Nate might not work at all if this so-called

Slim Porter were not found and brought into the plot quite soon. He settled down to wait.

Twenty minutes later, Bloke returned. There were five possible *cantinas*. He had visited three of them, and knew for certain that Slim and his cronies had not been in any of them. That left the other two. Having done what he considered to be a reasonable search, he backtracked to the office to see how the reverend gentleman's patience was holding out.

Wil opened the door just before Bloke could get his hand on it, and lifted the startled fellow indoors. 'I'm here on business for a very important lady in this town. If she thought a small undersized young man like yourself was deliberately getting in her way she might do something desperate about you. Where is Porter?'

'I looked an' I didn't find him. I looked in Pedro's, in Juan's and in Conchita's. He wasn't in any of them. And they were not expectin' him. So, I came back to tell you, señor.'

'Why didn't you investigate Paco's an' Jorge's?'

Bloke gasped and almost fell off his stool. It had never occurred to him that a gentleman of the cloth could possibly know the names of the proprietors of all the town's Mexican *cantinas*. He started to gesticulate with his small hands, looking for the first time elegant in his communications.

'I feared for your patience, padre.'

'You should have feared for what might happen after my patience gave out, *amigo*. I'll go an' look myself. If I find that you have not been speaking the truth, I'll be back to take my revenge! *Comprende?*'

Bloke nodded slowly, and watched with a peculiar fascination as the visitor stalked off down the deserted street in the direction of the drinking-dens.

Negative in Paco's. Jorge's tough brother-in-law was slightly inebriated and deliberately obstructive. So, Slim had to be around somewhere. In the second of two officially empty adobe dwellings he found the man he sought snoring in an alcove, using the shade of a thick arched wall.

As soon as Wil saw him, he recognised him from years back. The nickname of 'Slim' was a misnomer. Porter was, in fact, considerably over fifteen stones in weight, and when he felt good quite proud of his bulk. Wil removed his dog-collar and went to work. First, he hauled the chap into a sitting position. Next, having failed to make any sense out of him, he threw water in his face. Porter stopped snoring, grumbled a bit, laughed and then subsided against the wall.

At this point, Wil lost his temper and decided to vary the treatment. In ordinary circumstances, he would have been gentle, even considerate, but now he felt that no sort of treatment could be barred. He banged Porter's skull against the wall a couple of times, achieved a change in the expression on the drunk's face, and then slapped him hard, first on one cheek and then on the other.

His temper was rising as his energy was being sapped. He never saw even the shadow of the person who struck him. The blow came from directly behind. It was hard and sure, and his senses left him just as surely as his spectacles flew off his head and came to rest in yellowed dog and hen meadow grass.

Bloke's return to the drinking-scene was the turning-point in the afternoon's events. He, it was, who immediately identified Slim's attacker as a visiting priest. Three Mexicans at once began crossing themselves and wondering whether a just retribution would catch up with them due to their treatment of a clerical person.

Bloke also was the one to think of a way out of their peculiar dilemma. He had

Slim jabbed in the posterior with some sort of a sailmaker's needle: the kind of treatment which even Porter could not take and stay stupefied. Slim managed to get to his knees, and while he was still annoyed about how he had been roused, Bloke was able to reason with him.

'This other fellow is the visitin' parson, the one from out of town. He came to the office bringing a special message an' he wouldn't be put off. I searched for you, and I failed to find you. Then the reverend came himself, and he was knockin' your head up to the wall when the *muchachos* relieved him of his senses. But it ain't good to knock out a priest.

'We ought to take him back to the office, Slim, an' deal with his message. This is the Grunbaums' big day, don't forget, an' if they're involved we could be in trouble.'

Porter grumbled and writhed and burped, but he recovered himself and helped to massage a bit of life back into Wil Coltman's limp frame. As soon as Wil started to recover, the three Mexicans withdrew and left all further dealings to the two from the telegraph office.

The sorry clergyman's senses seemed to come and go. He found himself on his feet with his hat jammed on his head. His legs were unreliable, but his long and short supporting henchmen made sure that he stayed on his feet.

His spectacles were smeared and evil smelling, as was his hat. Moreover, his jacket and trousers needed sponging. However, the trio continued with their hit-and-miss progress back to the telegraph office. In the last fifty yards, Wil's ability for constructive thought returned to him. He ignored the others' argument about who smelled the freshest and mulled over what he ought to do.

At the three short steps leading up to the office, the trio became disjointed. Wil flopped down hard. Bloke made a suggestion, but Porter waved his brawny arms about recklessly.

'You take the reverend into the office. *Me, I'll* go under the pump first. Then he can take a turn, if he feels like it.'

So saying, Slim reeled off round the back of the office, and Bloke opened the door for the visitor.

'I'll be all right, Bloke. See Slim gets back in here as soon as you can. Don't let him stretch out again. Remember, I have a little job for him.'

Bloke touched his hat and left Wil to his own devices. The latter moved indoors, produced from his pocket the message drafted out earlier. In the gloom, he found a regular signal pad and rapidly wrote on it with a thick black stub of pencil.

Copy this message on regular paper and deliver it to Mr Nate Grunbaum at once. The said N.G is likely to make trouble for S.P if he slips up on delivery.

Wil then pinned the message, the instruction and two one-dollar bills to the counter and slipped out of doors. From a nearby corner he witnessed the return of the ill-assorted partners. They entered, came out again and looked around, then re-entered. After a short interval, out they came having shared the dollars and sauntered off in search of Nate Grunbaum.

Wil then took his turn under the pump.

TEN

In the meantime, Charleen had circulated for a short while among the more staid and sober guests. She had forced herself to dance two more times with her 'husband' and taken her chances to slip away from him. One time she was earnestly in conversation with the bridesmaids and their parents. Another time, she was chatting with the peace officers, perspiring in their best suits. And then, quite unobserved, she was out of the door and threading her way through the town to the Mayer House, which in her private thoughts seemed to her like a sanctuary.

Charleen slipped in by the back door as Miriam and Lettie were entering at the front. The sisters were discarding their parasols and taking off their bonnets when

Charleen suddenly confronted them and gave each of them a warm hug.

'My, my, you're away from the festivities early,' Lettie blurted out haughtily.

'If you ask me, I'd say our little girl is not fully recovered from her condition of yesterday. And that reception is goin' to get noisier before it finally quietens down.' Miriam opined.

Charleen nodded and smiled. 'As a matter of fact, I still feel a bit unsettled. Sort of jumpy, if you know what I mean. I'd like a glass of milk, and a few hours quiet. If I'm not disturbed.'

Miriam produced the milk and ushered Charlie into her own bedroom.

'We'll play it by ear, as they say, Charlie,' the gentle sister advised. 'One thing your new husband is not likely to be on his wedding night. And that is, sober and quiet. Don't bother if he doesn't make it tonight, sweetie.'

'I'd feel better if he didn't,' Charleen replied frankly.

Nate Grunbaum liked nothing better than a fast gallop around the town, especially when he had partaken of a few alcoholic drinks. On this particular afternoon, Willie took it upon himself as the best man to try and keep all groups entertained. It was when he came to the group of young males nearest in temperament to himself that he finally abandoned his assumed manners and let himself go. Nate agreed with anxious readiness to his suggestion about borrowing a few good riding horses from a downtown livery, and there was no lack of young men willing to ride them.

Altogether, there were six starters. Roughly, they were supposed to ride around the perimeter streets a couple of times and finish up outside the hall. A restless farmer started them off. He then lost interest as they all went out of sight in a cloud of street dirt, headed for the north end.

By the time Slim Porter and his sidekick,

Bloke, emerged on the scene, the racing horses had become separated. All six riders were partially inebriated, and none of them cared too much about keeping to the stipulated route.

In an intersection on the south side of town, the clerk and his buddy were almost run down by two riders who accidentally came into contact with each other. Forking their mounts as if they were riding burros, a carrot-headed youth and a bulky fellow in a crumpled silk hat rode down the street like marauding guerillas.

Slim dived for cover under an awning while Bloke slipped under the steps of the nearest sidewalk. As soon as the pair had gone out of sight, the two came into view again, commiserating with each other and wondering whether the delivery of the message was as important as the padre had made out.

Bloke was for abandoning the project, but the sudden appearance of the man they sought, making a sharp turn out of the northernmost street and turning to ride towards them, restored their confidence again.

'That's him, Bloke, I'd swear it!'

'I sure believe you're right, Slim. Maybe we can stop him. Looks as if his saddle has slipped. He's in trouble anyways.'

Nate's dappled grey was not in as good shape as he had thought at the outset. Every now and then, it paused, blowing hard as if it expected its rider to dismount and do something about the saddle. Nate, however, ignored its protest and did all within his powers to keep it on the move. He had no idea where he was in relation to the finishing-spot, nor whether he led or was behind.

As Slim and Bloke cautiously positioned themselves across the street, intent upon stopping Nate for his own good, Wil Coltman fresh from the pump, appeared at a corner. He took in the scene and the probable development and ducked back out of sight, keen to witness the immaculate future on two counts.

Slim, who was of course much larger than his partner, moved forward confidently, at first spreading his arms and then waving his battered hat.

He called out hoarsely: 'Now hold on there, Mr Grunbaum, I've got an important message for you. Party said for it to be delivered without delay!'

As the grey horse dodged at the last minute, Bloke warned his friend not to hand over the wrong piece of paper. The grey came near to the beady-eyed dwarf, failed to panic him into running away and threw up its forelegs as the little man leapt in the air with his arms spread.

Nathan was the fall guy. He sailed over the grey's rump and landed heavily in the dirt with the dust settling around him, and his perspiration cooling. Bloke aimed a kick in the horse's direction and allowed it to go ahead, riderless.

A scattering of curious people took in the scene, but they backed away hurriedly as the wild young man coughed out fluent curses and attempted to focus on them. Slim and Bloke raised him between them. They dragged him to the nearest water-trough, and took turns in dipping his head in it until he recovered.

Eventually, he blinked and tested his legs. He was thankful when they supported his weight. 'Where's my horse? Is the race over? Did you say something to me, before the accident?'

'Don't you bother none about the state of the race, Mr Grunbaum. This here special message is a whole lot more important to you than winnin' a casual race around the town. You hear me? This is Slim. Slim Porter. I got this message for you. About the foal, I guess.'

Nate had the devil's own job, at first, in focusing upon the message, but he managed it after a while. The mention of the foal gave him the determination. He read it through, aloud.

'This is important. The most important

thing in my life today. Did you see which way my horse went? I've got to get back to my family, an' explain things. At the hall, you know.'

The helpful couple did a lot of nodding and supporting. Bloke found the runaway grey where Wil had tied it, and soon they had him back at the hall, where the musicians were beginning to sound as if they were wilting.

Ten minutes later, in one of the private rooms of the hall, Nate worked assiduously to improve his condition. Willie was there assisting, but the latter removed himself as soon as Grunbaum senior joined his son and started to look chagrined over his appearance. After the first parental outburst, Nate backed off, dried his hands and held up Slim's signal pad in front of Cy's face. Cy had to back off because he could no longer read things close without reading glasses.

'If only my son could prevent himself

from behavin' like a no-good bum, on his weddin' day of *all* days!'

However, Cyrus was full of curiosity and backed away to the window to take advantage of the sun's rays on the paper. It took a minute or more for the full impact of the message to sink in. Eventually, he looked up, studied his son's puffy face for a few seconds and knew that Nathan was keener on the foal business than he was upon the consummation of his marriage.

Nate moved around the room, drying himself and trying to make it seem casual as he tested his sprained ankle with all his weight on it. He was relieved when he found he could manage so long as he did not leave all his weight on it for too long.

'If this message is genuine, you'd have to set off tonight to be around in North Junction first thing tomorrow!'

'I know that, Pa,' Nate replied calmly.

'But you can't go tonight because you have to consummate your marriage. You *do* know what that means, don't you? You have to be with Charleen tonight!'

Nate stopped pacing. He threw aside the towel. After taking two or three deep breaths he felt strong enough to perpetuate the argument.

'I know it's usual, the thing to do an' all. But it ain't absolutely necessary in this particular case, Pa.'

'How are you an' Charleen different from all the other folks gettin' married, I want to know?'

Nate waved for his father to shut up. 'Charleen is not quite herself. She's not well. Something to do with women an' their condition, I suppose. So it wouldn't spoil her weddin' night if the sleepin' part of bein' married started one night later.'

Cy shook his fists. 'You can't presume on that sort of thing, son! Women set great store by the weddin' night. It's very special to them, even if they're too excited. Too excited to sleep!'

Nate puffed out his chest. 'It might be

kinder to let my wife sleep. Alone. Not thinkin' she's obligated, when she's unwell an' tryin' to hide it!'

Cy took over the pacing. He stuck his hands under the tails of his jacket and made them stick out like a cockerel's tail feathers.

'Even if she knew what you had in mind,' he resumed, 'even if she actually approved of what you intend to do, it wouldn't work. You ridin' through the night with that other young drunk, Willie Bridson! I tell you it wouldn't work, Nate. It's—it's impracticable.'

Nate folded his arms, paced and collided with his father. Cy caught his breath, wondered what sort of an argument this wilful son of his was going to put up next, and stepped unwillingly aside.

Nate grinned. 'It's not impracticable, Pa. We could go by rail.'

'Now I know the booze has got to you, son. We don't have a team to drive the loco. We gave them the time off, on

171

account of the wedding!'

This time, Nate positively beamed. 'That's where you're wrong, Pa. There's one item connected with this whole business you don't know about. The honeymoon! It was my intention to take Charleen aboard the private train. Spend the night on board, if she wanted to. Or go to one of the other towns, if she preferred. So, Gus Filbert, the loco engineer, is alerted and all ready for a trip. So is his fire-boy. So you see, it's a distinct possibility.'

For a change, Nate frowned.

He resumed: 'But there is a snag which needs to be ironed out.'

Cy, who had been agreeably surprised by the revelation about his private rolling stock being used for the bridal pair, suddenly blinked, and thought back over the rest of their argument.

'If you can convince Charleen like you've done me, Nate, you'll get away with it!'

Nate checked on his chin, wondering if

he ought to have a second shave that day. 'That's not my sort of job. It's where *you* come in, Pa. All you have to do is bring Ma up to date and ask her to go an' speak with the Rodwall sisters. Woman talk, that's what it needs. You'll see. Offer her some sort of gift for bein' such a good mother to the groom. Something like that, eh?'

Cy soon recovered from his son's eloquence. In his mind's eye he could see Kate's characteristic response to a request that she should go and parley with the Rodwalls. Land's sakes, Kate was bad enough at tactful diplomacy, but with the Rodwalls she never achieved the right sort of effect. Never!

'Oh, not that, son. Your mother will never do it. For goodness' sake! Kate and the Rodwalls don't get on. They *never* got on, ever! And that means I'll have to go round myself. Nate, if this wasn't your weddin' day you'd never get me to make so many sacrifices. Hell, I can't stand those spinsters either. Negotiating with them won't be easy.'

Nate gripped him by the shoulders. 'Just think what it will be like, Pa, if we pull it off. The Grunbaums will have the fastest up-an'-comin' colt in the whole of the county. Maybe further afield, too. We could take our animals to other parts by rail. I never thought of that before.'

'You an' your ambitions. Sometimes you bother me, Nate. Get me a glass of that punch, if there's any left. If I don't get goin' straight away I'll never make it to the Mayer house.'

Five minutes later, Grunbaum senior left. Kate waylaid him on the way out, but when he explained that an alternative to his visiting the Mayer house was for her to go instead, she capitulated and told him to hurry about his business.

To his complete surprise, Cy found it all too easy to persuade the Rodwall sisters that the first night of the bride and groom should be postponed. They were so co-operative that he had a distinct impression that they had willed it to turn out that way. He came away again wondering if they could read thoughts, or whether they had some sort of witchcraft training that the town did not know about.

Full of his good news, he hastened back again to the hall, but he found that his son and Willie Bridson had taken his efforts all for granted. They had changed into ordinary cattlemen's outfits while he had been away. Furthermore, Filbert, the engineer, and his young negro fire-boy had already arrived.

Filbert said: 'We've had a head of steam up for the last half-hour, Mr Nate. We didn't think you'd leave the proposed trip too late.'

The engineer was brimming over with enthusiasm about the trip, but his outlook changed when he heard the bride would not be travelling.

ELEVEN

Still wearing the guise of a reverend gentleman, Wil began to make his preparations for leaving South Loop City where he had performed his most spirited and critical acting performance to date. Although he was tired of the subterfuge, he maintained his gait, his stance and all the other little mannerisms as he went through his leaving routine.

His visit to the livery presented no difficulty. Charleen had her own riding horse, and no one made any to-do about her occasionally demanding to have it saddled and run out at an unusual hour. Not even when a visiting priest requested it, at the same time as he collected his own horse. Wil paid for the keep of the leggy roan, signed for Charlie's bay gelding, and took the two mounts in the direction of the Mayer house. On the way, he made two slight detours in case anyone was showing an unhealthy interest in his latest movements.

Leaving the horses hitched to the rail alongside of the house, Wil flitted round to the back door. No sooner had he knocked on it than Charleen presented herself, putting her finger to her lips to check any loud conversation. The girl had already made sure that the Rodwalls stayed away from the door while she made her covert departure. When she would be back, she did not know. Nor did she know how her relationships would be affected by the day's events.

Wil whipped off his spectacles. 'Are you ready to go, Charlie? I have the horses round the side.'

Her long auburn hair was tied back in a pony-tail at the nape of her neck. On her head she wore a light-coloured, flat-crowned, stiff-brimmed stetson. Her shapely figure still showed under a grey shirt, a padded vest of the same colour and denims.

'Sure, Wil. I'll get my few things.'

Side by side, and acting furtively, they tiptoed round the corner of the house and stowed the girl's belongings into the saddle bags. She noted that Wil was wearing his .45 Colt and that his Winchester .73 was in his saddle scabbard.

As they peered around, anxiously checking whether anyone was watching their doings, Charleen said: 'How long before dark, Wil?'

He gestured, indicating the gathering shadows. 'Less than half an hour, Charlie. Don't get worried. Cy's liquor has done a lot to dull people's senses. I figure many folks will retire to bed early tonight. We have one short call to make, then we'll ride clear of town.'

He boosted her into the saddle, felt her shudder as their bodies touched and wondered if she was really fearful, or if the evening chill was affecting her. The short ride to Marta Hickstead's shack on the south-eastern extremity seemed to take hours.

Marta was standing up behind her chair, exercising her legs and working up to going indoors. Between them, they manoeuvred her off the verandah and saw to her immediate needs. Wil returned his borrowed gear to the chest of the late actor. He thanked her, asked her not to mention what he had been doing that day, and eventually managed to leave.

In her bed, with a hot drink, Marta called her farewells, and told them not to stay away as long in the future. They made their responses and rode away again. Wil's keenness not to be apprehended in town made Charlie thoughtful. He looked a keen, tough, self-confident young man transformed by his high-crowned, Texas-rolled stetson and black bandanna. She would have been more surprised had she known about the way in which he had beaten off the trail ambush as he started out from Clearwater.

Eventually, the buildings, the trees and all the trappings of the settlement thinned out and dropped behind them.

'You—er—you decided it would be best to go to Bitter Creek first, Charlie. No doubt to spend some time with your friend—Abigail?'

'Abigail Brace,' Charlie replied. 'Shop assistant. Thirty-six years of age. A spinster. I don't know yet what I'll have to ask of her, but I do know she's friendly and absolutely loyal.'

Wil was slow to answer. 'I suppose she'll be a friend in need. And if she's not at home, there'll be others.'

'She'll be at home,' Charlie assured him confidently.

There were lots of things Wil would have liked to discuss with Charlie, but the day had been long and he was tired. Moreover, he wanted to give his attention to the trail as the darkness deepened. The moon was pale, and the stars high. They heard a coyote howling about a half-hour later, and shortly after that Charlie shivered.

In spite of all her past experience on horseback, she had not done much riding by night. It was not particularly cool, but nevertheless the dwindling temperature got through to her due to the lightness of her clothing.

'Pull over here, Charlie,' Wil instructed.

When she had done so, he unstrapped his thick padded jacket and insisted that she should wear it for the rest of the journey. She was grateful, and—wrapped up in her thoughts again—she found herself comparing his thoughtfulness with the sort of treatment she had received and would still get from a spoiled, self-centred fellow like Nate Grunbaum.

Another couple of miles went by. And still Charlie was not fully at ease. Wil checked the roan a little and rode closer to her.

'If there's anything I can do, I hope

you'll say about it,' he murmured.

'Wil—I—would you think it foolish of me if I asked you to ride double with me for a while? I know I'm bein' childish, but I get to thinkin' if there's life behind the trailside boulders an' scrub.'

Wil chuckled. He found it easier so to do since he threw away the pads he had used to fill out his face. 'Your horse or mine, *amigo?*'

It was quite an interesting manoeuvre, getting Charlie off the back of her bay gelding onto the saddle of the roan without dismounting. For a second or two, they thought that they were about to lose their balance and drop to the track, but Wil shifted adroitly and the roan made an intelligent adjustment which righted everything.

Neither horse seemed to appreciate the move, but the bay was the first to recover and take on its lighter duties at the rear. Wil hugged his passenger who leaned against him murmuring gratefully.

The progress was slower. Inevitably, the roan tired and the change over to the bay had to be made.

'Too bad we have to keep running away, Wil. Otherwise, we could have a fire and simply wrap up for the rest of the night.'

'In any other circumstances, I would welcome such a suggestion, Charlie, but havin' taken so many chances with your affairs I can't let you down now. We must go on.'

The bay took on the hard labour, and for a time Charlie dozed in the saddle. Wil kept his heavy eyelids working, but only with an effort. Eventually, it was the bay which prompted him to change the mode of travel about a half-mile away from Bitter Creek. He knuckled his eyes, gently massaged Charlie into wakefulness and pointed ahead to where the slumbering town still showed the light of a few fitful lamps used to attract late-night business.

'You want me to come into town with you, Charlie? See you to the door? It wouldn't be any trouble.'

'Any other time I'd say yes, but not tonight, Wil. I'm obliged to you. I'll ride on. You hold back a bit. Maybe it would be better if I don't know where you're going. Don't answer that.'

Wil dismounted. He held the bay while the girl stood in the stirrups and rubbed her tired lower limbs. She murmured: 'It seems so final, sayin' farewell to a fellow-rider in the middle of the night. I'll be all right, of course. But neither of us can say when we'll meet again, can we?'

Wil thought about it, stared up into her face and shook his head.

'You know you can deny everything when the time comes, Charlie,' he informed her earnestly. 'Nothing will make me implicate you in what I've done. I never realised at the outset that—that buying time was goin' to put people on the rack. Even now, my brother is nowhere around and, apparently, not interested. Maybe it's a good thing we can't read the future, eh?'

'We'll have to agree on that, Wil. At the present, I'm still a free agent. Perhaps with obligations. Anyway, let's say *adios* for now. And give me a kiss before you go.'

One stretched up, the other stretched down. *'Hasta la vista,* Charlie. I'll be seein' you. Ride carefully, you hear?'

'You too, *amigo.* And here's to an improvement in the Bollard fortunes. Good luck!'

The efforts of the bay soon put a useful gap between them. Wil mounted up and watched the darkness gradually smudging Charlie's outline. He wanted to shout after her that he would do it all again if she wanted, but strong doubts and a yearning after something he wasn't clear about kept him quiet.

He would have been surprised and pleased if he had known that Charlie was feeling just as weak, and wanting to call back that she might very well need him to help her again.

As always 'Moose' Malone, or Bloke, as he had come to be known in South Loop, had a lot of time on his hands. The day of the wedding was one of seeming revelations to him. He had noted something different about the visiting reverend's manner as soon as the priest arrived at the telegraph office. Not long after that, the transformation of the said priest into a rather wild punch-throwing unpeaceful operator during the search for Slim Porter had truly impressed him.

Having said enough to get the un-conscious holy man restored to his senses and put on his feet again, Bloke felt he had a special interest in the travelling man's stay, and in his future. Consequently, as he wandered the town in the early evening, covertly spying and occasionally scrounging, he kept a special look-out for the Reverend Eli, and for those involved in the wedding.

For a time, he hovered about in the entrance to the hall, but someone or another who thought his unique appearance would bring ill luck to the marriage pushed a bottle of wine into his hands and ushered him off the premises to drink it elsewhere.

He did not express any surprise at his treatment. During his brief sojourn in the vestibule, he had seen enough to know that the gathering lacked several of the key figures in the day's celebrations. Nate Grunbaum had cleared off with his sidekick, Bridson. And the bride had also made her excuses and left. So had the slightly mysterious parson.

If only Slim would not booze so much in the evenings, he would have somebody with whom to discuss the more significant events which few people seemed to know about. A systematic search for the elusive Slim placed Bloke quite near to the Mayer house at the time when the mysterious stranger with the two horses arrived.

By straining his eyes, he noted a few details about the horse toter. Furthermore, the person who came out dressed for riding was definitely a female. A young female with long straight hair. And, coming from that particular house, it was almost certain that she was Charleen Grunbaum, Nate's bride of a few hours.

Slim was a widower, and Bloke did not have any hankering towards marriage himself. Nevertheless, he had an ordinary man's curiosity about weddings and the way the principals conducted themselves, and he was absolutely assured that Charleen ought to have been with Nate. She wasn't. She had gone off with a man bringing her a horse. And Nate, himself, had hightailed it on an urgent errand which took him off by railway train towards North Junction.

The priest was involved not only in the wedding ceremony, but also in the delivery of the telegraph message. So he ought to be about somewhere, but he did not seem to have the knack of joining in with the others celebrating the marriage.

There were shouts and fighting going in two of the town's saloons in spite of the free drinks on issue from the hall, and Bloke sagely avoided getting involved with those trading punches. Every now and then, he took a good swig out of his wine-bottle, gargled with it and swallowed slowly. He had heard in his youth that it was good for the throat, the larynx and other organs adjacent to the throat.

Around ten o'clock, as he still wandered the streets, he started to shout the name of his friend and associate. To his surprise, at the third bout of shouting, the unmistakable hoarse voice of the man he sought called back to him.

The voice came from the back of a portable wooden water-trough close up against a sidewalk. Some time earlier, Slim had sought the trough to freshen himself, or someone who did not like him had tried to duck him in it. Either way, Slim had not profited by the trough waters. He had missed his way at the last moment and fallen: to become jammed due to his bulk behind it.

Bloke looked down upon him, at first puzzled and then mildly amused. Slim was trapped by the shoulders and his head. His vintage hat was still on his head, but the sides of the brim were flattened down over his ears affording a protection and at the same time causing the head to be wedged.

'Shame on you, Slim. Tut, tut. I've been lookin' for you for hours, an' all the time you've been hidin' away from me at the back of a horse-trough. Sometimes, I think you don't care for me at all. If you'd been a bit more friendly, instead of slipping off on your own we could have gone to the festivities together and enjoyed ourselves. Instead of that, you wind up on your own and I get frustrated lookin' for you. You want a drink of my wine?'

Slim attempted a frustrated roar of anger, but it came out muted because of his trapped head. Bending close, Bloke heard him protest.

'Just—just get me out of here, will you? I'm in pain. We'll talk about other things later.'

Slim groaned, sometimes quietly, at other times noisily. Bloke, on his knees, and peering under the trough, decided that he was probably in pain, and not just feeling sorry for himself.

'All right, hold on a minute, pard. I'll get you loose!'

Bloke exercised his latent cruelty in the way he slowly wrenched the flattened hat away from his partner's head. By that time, they were both breathless and Slim's shoulders were still not moving. Bloke retreated, using the hat to take some water out of the trough. He then tipped the liquid generously over his friend's head and shoulders and only told him about the slime and foreign bodies in the trough when he had drunk some of it to cool his tongue and throat.

Eventually, the high fellow slid out feet first and squatted on the sidewalk steps until he recovered his breath and his equilibrium.

In the meantime, Bloke poured into his apparently willing ears all his notions about the groom, the bride and the mysterious travelling priest. Slim was curious, as anyone would have been knowing the set-up, but he was slow to come to conclusions. Bloke despaired of him repeating what he had just heard and only altering the bovine expression on his face.

Bloke bullied him about his thought processes: so much so that he tried to sum up what he had heard. 'I believe you, Bloke. Nate's gone to North Junction without his bride. His bride, so you say, has dressed up for the trails an' gone for a ride with a stranger, an' the priest may be a prize-fighter or somethin' just occasionally doin' a reverend's job. I'm *interested*, Bloke. Don't be put off. But you know me. I need to sleep some. We'll talk about the weddin' folks again tomorrow, huh? Now, if you ain't willin' to assist me back to the office I'll have to doss down here, but bein' wet makes a man cold before his time an' that don't figure with me.'

Bloke cursed him quietly, pocketed his wine-bottle and went through the motions of getting Slim on his feet before it was too late. The journey back to the office was long and tiring. On the way, the dwarf went through Slim's pockets to see if he had had an expensive day. He was not impressed with what he found in them.

TWELVE

That night so significant to so many people in and around South Loop City slowly and inexorably ticked away. Morning came, as usual.

In the Railway Hotel, North Junction, a waiter in a striped shirt knocked crisply on the door of Nathan Grunbaum on the first floor. Without waiting for a reply, the fellow entered, crossed the floor and opened the drapes. While he was pouring out coffee on the food trolley, Nate enquired sleepily about the time.

'Just turned six o'clock, sir. The time you asked for. The coffee is pipin' hot. We can provide any sort of food you may want in a few minutes. That is, if you can let me have the order right now.'

Towards the end of the waiter's deliberations, Nate remembered where he was and why he had gone there. 'Just so, just so. No, on this day of all days I think I'll forgo my usual hearty breakfast and make myself ready for business. If you'll just make sure my friend next door is out of bed, I'll be obliged. Thank you.'

Nate tossed a half-dollar piece onto the trolley, indicated that he had no other needs and waved the attendant out of the room.

Fifteen minutes later, he was out of the hotel and pushing his reluctant sidekick, Willie Bridson, ahead of him.

Topping his smart tailored riding-shirt, Nate wore a neat padded sleeveless vest, the pockets of which were on the inside. He always wore this particular garment when he had a big money transaction in hand. At the Rottenberg residence, a tall mannish middle-aged spinster housekeeper answered the door, and managed to unbend when the two cowpuncher persons doffed their hats and asked if it would be possible to see Mr Rottenberg on a matter of business.

The woman blinked hard, cocked her head on one side, decided that he was perfectly serious, and then smiled nervously. 'Why, I couldn't rightly say, young man. As the master is out of town, you'd have to travel to where he's gone. As a matter of fact, I don't rightly recollect his destination. Wouldn't your business keep until he returns?'

Nate tried to avoid showing that he was put out. 'Well, no, I—er—I wouldn't have thought so. It has to do with livestock, and a rather pricey sale.' He patted himself over the heart and produced from the pocket hidden in that region a faint crackle of crisp bank-notes. 'Are you *sure* Mr Rottenberg isn't at home? If I've called too early, I'll be only too glad to come back later. You only have to say.'

The caller beamed, but the servant kept a straight face. Down the wide ornate staircase came the booming voice of the mistress of the house. Mrs Rottenberg had brought with her a strong Scandinavian accent a good score of years ago: an accent which she had not tried very hard to lose.

'Who is that, Hortense? If he wants the master, tell him he'll have to go to El Paso to the bankers' conference. And if he doesn't take himself away from my door I'll have the shotgun toter come round from the back area to encourage him! Let me know if I have to use the voice-pipe!'

All the much-practised Grunbaum ill humour and temper was rapidly asserting itself on account of the overpowering voice of the mistress. Nate never liked losing face, particularly in front of his cronies, men like Willie Bridson. However, he kept his temper with an effort and tried to put into words some of his hostile feelings.

'Well, now, Hortense, we seem to be at cross-purposes. That peculiar-sounding Scandinavian person surely is not up to date. I'll think of a better way of communicating. Your mistress doesn't sound to be the type to need a shotgun to watch over her. How old will she be? Sixty?'

He laughed roguishly, touched his hat and casually walked away from the building knowing that the housekeeper would relay what he had said about the mistress. Willie's scowl confirmed that it had not been a wise thing to do, being rude to the horse breeder's wife, but Nate was still feeling good and anticipating the sort of day in which his dreams and ambitions would be boosted very considerably.

'You didn't visit the Rottenberg corral that other time, did you, Willie? Well, that's where all the action is. It's my belief that cunnin' Swede is deliberately startin' rumours about his present whereabouts to put off folks he don't want to do business with!

'Hell, a bankers' conference in El Paso! What do they take us for? You keep in step with me, Willie boy. I'll show you the mare an' the foal, an' when I get goin' raisin' first-class horse-racin' stock I'm goin' to give you a useful position in my new organisation. You mark my words.'

Willie had his doubts about his own business acumen, but he kept them to himself. As he massaged his bent Roman nose and kept his steps in line with his partner's, he reflected that he had learned a good deal of horse 'lore' from his father, an Army farrier. But nothing he had done since he came of age had suggested a businessman's brain.

The approach track to the remote Rottenberg corral was neatly pruned back and trimmed. Half-way along it, a signpost suggested that anyone having gone that far without specific business to attend to ought to turn about without further delay.

Nate laughed, and lengthened his stride. Willie became slightly breathless. When they left South Loop they had travelled prepared for most ordinary emergencies, but on this little jaunt they had left behind their gun-belts and revolvers. Not that they were likely to be robbed by Rottenberg personnel. It was just a feeling which Willie had that the negotiating might not be as straight forward as Nathan thought.

'Money talks, *amigo*. The almighty dollar, in note form. Clean an' crisp an' in large numbers always melts the hearts of those who love *dinero*.'

Willie nodded and kept his peace. He was still further out of breath when the Rottenberg corral came into view. In appearance, it was more like an army stockade for recalcitrant prisoners than an ordinary work-out area for promising riding stock. It had solid wooden walls to a height of six feet topped with poles and barbed wire. A gate of similar material was closed. While they were wondering about access, a tall poker-faced guard in a grey Texas-style hat and double-breasted hide jacket suddenly bobbed up a little to one side of the gate and looked down on them. The muzzle of his shoulder weapon rested on a strand of wire.

'Good day to you, stranger. The boss don't have no business appointments today, so I have to stick to the rules an' advise you to git back the way you came. Without delay.'

He levered a bullet into the barrel, clicked his tongue and nodded neutrally without altering his facial expression.

Nate squared his shoulders and set his feet apart. 'I was here before. With Mr Rottenberg. I didn't have any trouble with guards on that occasion.'

'If the boss brought you in, we wouldn't even enquire your name, mister. Today is different.'

'I'll say it's different,' Nate grumbled. 'I've come all the way from South Loop in my Pa's private train to see your boss about a mare called Cascade or somethin' like that. An' a new foal named Flyin' Spray, I guess.'

The guard failed to show the sudden inspirational interest which Nate's revelations were intended to promote. He cleared his throat.

'Now see here, mister. We just guard the place. We don't know about any special deals. The animals are all in numbered boxes an' stalls an' that's about all I'm entitled to tell you. Except the time of day.'

This time the guard deliberately looked away. Nate dug his fists into his pockets and wished he had brought with him his revolvers. On occasions like this, a man felt naked without them.

'I figure you're entitled to one more polite piece of talk, guard. Call the boss an' I'll forget you've held me up far longer than is necessary.'

Someone whistled. On the far side of the wooden wall, two or three angry dogs ran to the gate. A voice said: 'You want I should open the dog-flap, Silas?'

Willie backed away from Nate, and

prepared to break into a run.

The guard said: 'No. We have a jasper here wants me to call the boss back from El Paso about some flyin' spray. Could you credit that? I guess it keeps the day from gettin' borin'.'

This further mention of El Paso deflated Nate like nothing else could. 'Something's wrong. Something's wrong, I tell you, guard. I had this tip-off from a friend. It was genuine. Mr Rottenberg is probably on his way back from El Paso at this very moment.'

The guard pointed his rifle and casually fired a bullet which ripped up soil between Nate's boots. Willie took off and did not wait to encourage his companion. Nate choked down his wrath and dodged off backwards, and then he turned about and ran speedily, overtaking Willie in some twenty yards.

A hundred yards away, Nate tried to put his venomous thoughts into words, but failed on account of breathlessness.

Eventually, he contrived a few words through his teeth. 'Some jasper is goin' to pay for this, Bridson, you mark my words.'

The Reverend Eli Broadburn began his important journey from the remote be-tween-towns rest-cabin at around half-past seven in the morning. Until just after nine o'clock he had with him his guards, Jake and Bluey Kimberley, who had treated him well during his stopover and put his mind at rest about the business of the wedding being delayed by twenty-four hours on account of the intended bride's indisposition.

On balance, although he had secret reservations about being an itinerant priest in this part of the world, he felt that he had been reasonably well treated this far, and that his work in South Loop would give him a reputation of sorts with the local populace, even though his efforts were always likely to pale into insignificance when compared with the flock shepherding of his formidable cousin, Abraham.

On the run-in to South Loop, he glanced at his watch and saw that it was nine-fifteen. Time for the couple bent on marriage to be out of their beds and coping with the last-minute jitters. Although he had never contemplated marriage himself, he had seen many young people before, during and immediately after the ceremony to know that their behaviour was often a little bit off-key.

South Loop was smoking gently, although there were few fires lit at that time of the morning. Eli produced from his pocket a small rectangular mirror in a leather case and studied his reflection at close quarters. His silver-framed spectacles concealed slight bags beneath his eyes. His dark suit looked dusty, and his straggle of grey beard would have looked more stylish had it been shortened a little. But couples bent on wedlock tended to overlook minor details.

He put the mirror back in his pocket, smiled to himself and coaxed his shaft-horse into a slightly greater effort.

A short way clear of town, he called to an urchin fishing in a shallow stream.

'Can you direct me to the church where the Grunbaum weddin' is to take place, lad?'

The boy in question took the stalk of grass out of his mouth, eyed the priest with an expression rounded with curiosity, and chuckled to himself.

'Just keep drivin' through the middle, reverend. You'll see it stickin' up higher than the other buildings. You're late for the wedding, though.'

Eli acknowledged and drove on, dismissing the lad's remark as being a mistake due to a dull mind. Outside the church, coloured paper streamers were tangled in the shrubbery. There *had* been a wedding. The lad had merely confused one wedding with another. The door was not locked. Here and there, he could detect minor traces of a ceremony having taken place but nothing to suggest the preparation for the Grunbaum affair. The town handyman, a rotund individual who had never really coped with American English since he left Poland, nevertheless directed Eli to the Grunbaum residence.

There he found Cy and Kate alone, dallying over a late breakfast out-of-doors and in the shade afforded by their verandah. They appeared to be a bit startled as he put the brake on and dismounted from the buckboard.

'Eli Broadburn. The Reverend Eli Broad-burn, at your service, dear Mr and Mrs Grunbaum. I trust my guesswork is accurate. How do you do?'

Kate stood up a fraction before Cy. Both were stunned.

Kate remarked. 'You can't be.'

Cy sounded more blunt. 'How can you be? The Reverend Eli was here yesterday. He performed our son's wedding! Besides, you don't look like Abe Broadburn at all. There ought to be some family resemblance.'

For once, Kate's glare had failed to close the lips of her husband.

The newcomer paused. He doffed his Quaker-style hat, dabbed the inner band and applied his handkerchief to his lined forehead.

'Madam, sir. In our profession it is not customary for one priest to intrude upon the work of another. Are you telling me a priest performed the wedding of Nathan Blackstone Grunbaum to Charleen Johnson Mayer, yesterday? In this town's church?'

Kate and Cy, unable to help themselves, talked at the same time, pouring out words all over him and merely confusing the issue. Eli firmly asked to see the groom, and was informed that he was out of town. After combing his beard for the fourth time with his long thin fingers, he argued.

'Is it then possible for a man of the cloth

to make contact with the bride? Or is she out of town, too?'

His voice sounded deadly, waspish almost. Kate and Cyrus eyed each other. They came to the conclusion that they would have to placate this extra clergyman by making an early visit to the Mayer house. Kate, a formidable woman herself, dreaded it. She had never ever bested the Rodwall sisters in a 'discussion' at any time. Side by side, they had her measure. As for Cy, in recent years he was becoming a late starter. At this hour of the morning, one chore he could have done without was acting as a mediator between the Rodwalls and his prickly wife.

Nevertheless, the two of them went meekly indoors, removed their padded dressing-gowns and donned a more modish form of dress intended for out-of-doors. Cy rumbled with indigestion. He elected to walk to the Mayer house, while Kate rode beside the new priest.

People called out to them, as they crossed the town. Enquiries were polite. Had they slept well, after their day of celebrating? Cy found it hard to reply politely. Kate ignored them, but Eli felt his stomach start to rumble again with a condition he had put down previously to unaccustomed trail travel.

As they entered the street where the Mayer house was, Kate showed a lot more tension. Eli spoke to her and she did not appear to have heard. Cy banged the knocker. Lettie answered the door. At first she merely showed surprise, but when she saw Kate hunched on the bench beside the man with the clerical collar her face clammed up. In answer to a call, Miriam joined her.

'Ladies, my wife an' I don't seek to bother you, but we have some sort of a misunderstanding. To assure this reverend gentleman about what happened yesterday, we'd like to see Charleen. Just for a minute or two. That's all.'

Visibly shaken, Eli Broadburn dismounted, and handed down Mrs Grunbaum who dearly wanted to stay where she was, on the buckboard.

Lettie remarked: 'Good day to you, sir. Mrs Grunbaum. We can't let you talk to Charleen because she ain't around. So sorry to disappoint you, I'm sure. You, in particular, reverend. You'll have had your visit for nothing.'

Kate's jaw dropped. She restored her expression with an effort. The reverend gentleman sagged against the gatepost. Cy found a point he could take up without going on the defensive.

'How come our daughter-in-law ain't here, an' we don't know anything about it? Huh?'

At that juncture, the mild-mannered Miriam began to assert herself. 'How come you are able to ask that, Cyrus Grunbaum, when your son preferred to take a train trip instead of bein' with his bride? Answer me that, if you can!'

'It was business, Miss Miriam. And it could have been put aside if Miss Charleen had been well enough to—er—go ahead. Er—all I can say is that I am surprised if Charleen is hidin' away from her new in-laws after so brief a time.'

'She's not hidin' away, Mr Grunbaum. She's out of town. No doubt on business. You're aware Charleen is a businesswoman in her own right, I do believe. What a pity the groom hasn't got some business of a tangible nature. It would have impressed the bride, and her closest associates, too.'

Kate stamped on the step. Cy, irked by her indignation, wanted to upgrade the Grunbaum prestige. 'If you'll tell us her immediate whereabouts, Miss Rodwall, we won't trouble you further.'

'We don't intend to give you her whereabouts, Mr Grunbaum, so that terminates the interview.' This was Lettie, who had stepped forward to take charge.

Eli Broadburn hesitated. All the conversation seemed to confirm that a wedding had taken place. The names mentioned were those of the two young people he was to have wedded. And that was that. Unless—unless the person who had conducted the service was not a proper clergyman.

While they were attempting to rally themselves for a retreat, reinforcements totally unexpected came to join them. Nathan was stepping it out manfully, really driving his boot heels into the dirt, while Willie toiled as usual a couple of strides behind him.

'What in tarnation are you doing round here, Pa? I've been lookin' all over for you since I got back from North Junction. Seems I've been duped. That hombre, Rottenberg, isn't aimin' to auction any foal. No foal has been born so far, an' that's the truth. So it seems I was taken out of town for no proper purpose. If you can't explain it, I'll have to talk seriously with Charleen. After all, she's involved an' I must do something about it.'

Kate was back on the seat of the buckboard, and the Reverend Eli had joined her. While Cy and Nate talked earnestly with their heads together, the grey-bearded parson coaxed the horse to leave the scene. He felt totally perplexed.

Willie waited, hands on hips, gradually recovering his breath. He was the first to see Miriam return to the Mayer front door with a shotgun held in a handy position for business. He wanted to blurt out a warning, but his voice was not yet ready for the effort.

Suddenly, Nate roared out in his best bullhorn voice. 'That answer may do for you, Pa, but I'm the groom, her husband, an' I demand to know more! Leave it to me!'

Nate took several purposeful strides towards the house, not comprehending what he saw. Miriam with the shotgun pointed at him did not register at first.

'Away with you, young man! Get your family business settled some other place than on our doorstep! You hear? Otherwise, I'll give you something to persuade you you won't like!'

Nate gasped. He came to a stop, feet apart and breathless. Another shoulder weapon pointed at him after a lapse of only a few hours. He looked round for help from Willie, but Bridson was prudently retreating around the first intersection.

'I demand to know where my wife is!'

Miriam closed the door, but the muzzle of the shotgun was immediately thrust through a slot-type letter-flap to continue its menace of the angry young man.

In less than a minute, Nate had withdrawn.

Some time later, over a painful meal produced by Grunbaum servants, the Reverend Eli and the Grunbaum family came to a conclusion difficult to credit.

The description of the clergyman who had performed the marriage, worked out from the many witnesses to the ceremony in the church, bore a very close resemblance to the man who had acted as a doctor to the Reverend Broadburn.

A few overheard remarks made by Eli's guards had led him to believe that the fellow he had believed to be a doctor was not a doctor at all, but another person who for some reason unknown had masqueraded as Bitter Creek's well-known physician.

If the fellow was not a doctor, then it was possible that the marriage had not been properly performed. A strong factor in the discussion was the way in which the mystery man had used the Reverend Eli's name to perform his duties.

As soon as the meal was concluded, Cy instigated several costly telegraph messages, asking questions in no fewer than six towns about the possibility of a known clergyman having taken Eli's place. The information was slow to come in, but when it did there was nothing at all to confirm that the other Eli was genuine.

Reluctantly, Broadburn informed his hosts that their son was not—as yet—married. Shortly afterwards, Nate withdrew to join Willie in a remote hostelry. After yesterday's high hopes, he now had no foal and no bride.

THIRTEEN

Rumours floating about the town had the effect of making Slim Porter, the beer-drinking telegraph clerk, produce a concerted effort to recollect some of the more unusual happenings of the last day or so. Across a rough wooden surface in a snack bar, where he and Bloke were taking their evening meal, Slim made an effort to get advice from his small partner.

After sinking a piece of bread soaked in beef gravy, Slim pointed with a long fat finger. 'You recollect what you told me the other evenin', about a man with two horses comin' to the Mayer house, an' a young female leavin'?'

'So what?' Bloke queried sullenly. 'Why are you interested now?'

'Could I tell Mr Nate without him askin' awkward questions about other things?'

The ill-assorted couple argued for a good ten minutes, putting in personal insults and gibes as if they hated each other. At the end of the meal, Slim trekked off to see Nate, with Bloke accompanying him a little distance behind.

In a private alcove of a local bar, Nate listened well although his head was thumping with the amount of liquor he had consumed since his retreat from the second firearm threat. He made Slim repeat everything he had said the first time, rewarded him with a two-bit piece and then dismissed him.

On the rear gallery of the Grunbaum residence, Nate found his father, who looked him over apprehensively.

'Sit down, son. What's new?'

Nate repeated what he had just heard, and summed up the situation as he saw it. 'I believe there's more to Charleen than we first thought. If you ask me, I'd say she's eloped with a jasper we don't know about. How do you see it?'

Cy poured him a drink, and offered him a small cigar which he took and lighted. 'It's possible, of course, but it don't do to jump to conclusions. If she's gone off with a man, on horseback, at a late hour, that looks and sounds suspicious. You're *right* to feel suspicious, son. It was your wedding day, and it didn't all go as it should have done. Charleen may have had bad advice from those two rascals, the Rodwall sisters.

'But, havin' said so much, we could be absolutely wrong. Charleen has business interests in several towns. If she had decided at a late hour to make contact with one of her managers, she would need an escort to look after her on the trails. Especially durin' the night hours. Do you agree?'

Nate shook his head several times and held back his answer, but in the end he had to agree with Cy's reasoning.

'You'll want to do a bit of horse ridin' yourself. After all, you have an instant right to find out where she is an' what she's up to. Even if the parson wasn't a real clergyman an' the weddin' didn't really take place. More so, in fact.

'Tomorrow mornin' you run out your best horse, take along Willie maybe, an' one or two of the other young jaspers in your group. Seek out the managers of the South-Western Traders' stores. Start with the ones we know. Levoloski is out, of course. But in Bitter Creek, there's a youngish woman with a bit of authority. Abigail Bruce, or something like that.'

'Gail Brace,' Nate put in casually. 'About thirty-six years old.'

'That's right,' Cy approved. 'If you fail there, you can try George Masters, the general manager. He runs the store in Newell. Everything will be all right. A girl like Charleen wouldn't simply go off into the blue leavin' behind a string of shops like she owns. She'd be bound to tell someone, otherwise she wouldn't be human. See what I mean?'

Nate nodded. He agreed with his father's reasoning and, for once, he had to admit that talking to Cyrus had done him good.

By working their horses fairly hard, Nate Grunbaum, Willie Bridson and a couple of back-up riders reached Bitter Creek before noon. Leaving the back-up pair to see to the needs of the horses, Nate and Willie went along to the store which Charles owned, and which was managed by Abigail Brace.

Nate went in first. He crossed the floor on tiptoe and abruptly pulled aside the Indian curtain which screened off a small private retiring-room which held a table, two chairs, a mirror and a few shelves.

Gail Brace was in there making entries in a large ledger when the curtains parted to show Nate's tense face. Gail had her long black hair in plaits. Her costume was a simple dark buckskin tunic along the lines of those worn by Indian squaws. She also wore cotton trousers and moccasins. A sudden frown sharpened the look in her blue eyes and accentuated her strong jaw-line.

'This is one part of the shop which is barred to customers, sir. I'd be obliged if you'd withdraw.'

Gail turned away from the intruder and carried on writing. After a few seconds' hesitation, Nate complied with her request. They next met across a counter neatly heaped with Indian rugs.

'Now, sir, what is your special interest?'

'Charleen Mayer, the owner. She left South Loop at a late hour last evenin' without intimatin' where she was goin'. I'm Nathan Grunbaum, and I'm lookin' for her. I'm impatient.'

Gail did not like Nate. She had only seen him once or twice before this encounter. As she knew her revelations would not please him very much, she smiled as she divulged.

'I see, Mr Grunbaum. Well now, Miss Mayer, she's impatient, too. She came here at a late hour last night, and she moved on again at an early hour this morning. There's no knowing when she will be satisfied with her tour of the shop circuit. My best advice is to ride to Newell. There, you will probably contact Mr George Masters, the general manager. He usually has a better idea than any of us what Miss Charleen has in mind. Now, is there anything *I* can do personally?'

'Do you really think Charleen might be in Newell, talkin' with Mr Masters?'

'It's a distinct possibility, Mr Grunbaum. And if you want coffee before you ride on there's a good place fifty yards down the street. On the left. Now, if you're *sure* there's nothing I can get you, I'll go back to my accounts. Good day to you.'

Nate wanted an argument, but there was nothing he could argue with Abigail about. So, hesitantly, he touched his hat, and wandered out into the street. Willie ceased to prop up a wall and fell into step beside him as he strode off heavy-footed, down the sidewalk.

'She ain't here, then. I thought as much.'

'She's been an' gone, Willie. Probably gone on first thing this morning to Newell, to talk with the general manager. Don't you think she ought to have told *me* before she cleared off like she did?'

'You're darned right, I do, Nate. It's almost as if she's avoidin' you. I didn't like to say earlier, but that's the way it looks to me.'

Nate glared at him. 'That bein' so, we'll take an hour off, get something to eat, an' then ride for Newell.'

Willie nodded. His heart was not in the search. Riding throughout the hottest part of the afternoon searching for a young woman who did not want to be found was not his idea of an overdue siesta.

George Masters was back at his base that same morning by ten-thirty. He was a flexible, self-disciplined man who could switch his plans for the day with remarkable ease. Wil Coltman's unexpected return in the middle of the night to Clearwater had surprised the general manager when he was awakened around seven o'clock.

He left Wil sleeping soundly in the back room, a note having been left out to intimate that Wil was willing to take back his responsibility at once. As Wil was thoroughly reliable, and George wanted to get back to his own establishment, he left a few messages with Merle Brisson and young Carlos, and cleared out directly after an early breakfast.

As a certain old clock was sounding off for eleven o'clock, Charleen walked a tired saddle-horse up the street and angled it over towards the hitch-rail near the South-Western Traders' store. She hitched it, slackened off the saddle and walked heavy-footed into the shop. Just as she did so, Masters was stoking his first pipe of the day behind the long counter.

For a few seconds, he seemed to be absolutely disconcerted, and then his lined face broke out in a smile of real pleasure.

'Why, Charlie! Miss Charleen, that is, to what do I owe the pleasure of this unexpected visit? I thought you'd be miles away, startin' out on your honeymoon with that up-an-comin' young Grunbaum fellow. Is anything wrong?'

The young woman moved up close to greet him. She gave him a hug and backed off slowly. 'I'm not on a honeymoon, as you can see. I needed to see you, to talk to you, George. As I'm not so sure of myself at the moment, maybe you could leave the shop to your assistant.'

The assistant came back from an errand, and George at once surrendered the immediate running of the store and took Charleen out on the back verandah. He smoked his pipe, and Charlie sipped a fruit drink.

'The wedding didn't go exactly as the Grunbaums had planned it, George.

Firstly, the Reverend Abe Broadburn couldn't perform, because he was unfit. A man who claimed to be his cousin did the ceremony. I was mildly indisposed. Other things happened. Nathan, the groom, went off in a hurry by rail to see about a much-sought-after foal which will probably win races when it grows up.

'While Nathan was out of town, I slipped away with the assistance of the man who continued the service.'

Masters revealed by the way he sucked his pipe how pleased he was that something had gone wrong with the Grunbaum wedding plans. He moved up and down on the edge of his seat, and only suppressed his excitement with a profound effort.

'Are you tellin' me that a priest helped you to be away from your bridegroom on the first night of your wedding?'

'Something like that, George. As a matter of fact, there's a mystery surrounding the—er—my priest. It is possible he may be an impostor. Not a priest at all!'

Masters suddenly guffawed. He coughed, gagged on his tobacco smoke and had to be patted on the back.

'Hell an' tarnation, Charlie, I do believe you're pleased not to be married to that young Grunbaum. I really do. Where's the priest, anyway?'

'I don't know exactly. What I would like to have explained is why you missed my wedding and a few other details, my man!'

'You know why,' Masters argued easily. 'Because I couldn't bear seein' you married to Grunbaum. So, I gave myself an excuse. A young man, just finishin' his probation as manager in Clearwater, Coltman by name, needed a day or two off. So I took over his store to let him go. I had a feelin' he wanted to go to South Loop. You didn't see him at the weddin', did you?'

Charleen puckered her brow. 'I don't believe I know anyone named Coltman. What did he look like, George?'

Masters tamped down his pipe. 'Oh,

tall, fair, blue-eyed. Kind of distinguished-lookin'. Carries a light beard and moustache. Age, about twenty-seven, I'd say. Smokes cigars, rides nicely.'

Gradually, Charleen's cupid's bow lips had rounded into a generous 'O'. Understanding was dawning in her troubled green eyes, bringing back enthusiasm and possibly hope. 'Does he have a way of putting his head on one side an' lookin' at you with a quizzical smile? Is there a bit chipped out of one of his front upper teeth? Does he have a habit of tilting small cigars at the corner of his mouth?'

Masters had started to nod, almost as soon as Charleen started her appraisal. Eventually, she rocked on her chair, hugged her knees and chuckled infectiously.

'That's my priest! That Wil Coltman of yours is my Wil Bollard. His father was once my guardian. Oh, you'll never know how pleased I am to learn that Wil Bollard was already workin' for South-Western Traders before he came to my weddin'.

So he's in Clearwater, right now, sleepin' off his exhaustion.'

Masters withdrew his pipe from his mouth in order to have a good uninhibited laugh. It was clear that Charleen had a lot more time for Wil Coltman—as he knew him—than she had for Nate Grunbaum. And, having given Wil a spell of leave, he felt that he was in the plot which had developed through Wil's resourcefulness as an actor. But where would it end?

'Oh, yes, he's in Clearwater, all right. But knowin' him, I'd say that by now he's finished sleepin' an' applied himself to store-keepin' again. Are you plannin' on seein' him right away?'

Charleen stood up and started pacing. 'Right away, George. I'm sure you understand the implications. We had to con Nate to get him out of town. As soon as he knows I've gone on my travels, he'll be right on my tail. Which probably means I have very little time in hand. If you can, when he comes along, try an' distract him.

I'd like for him to look for me elsewhere, till I have time to work out what I'm goin' to do. If I drop out of circulation for a while, I know I can rely on you to keep the chain still workin', George. That's a great help. Do you think you could get me a change of horse while I seek a bite to eat?'

Masters nodded and approved. As a result of his efforts, Charleen rode out of town less than half an hour later on a fresh horse.

Wilbur Coltman Bollard arose towards noon the following day. The long hard ride to Clearwater had taken most of the stamina out of his riding horse which had already been tired by the time he reached the parting of the ways short of Bitter Creek. Fortunately, the animal was quite reliable, and Wil felt sure that it would be given a long lay-off before being called upon to perform in such a protracted way again.

His two loyal supporters awoke him quite a time after he had anticipated being roused. They avoided any suggestion of criticism, and were quite intrigued when he told them he had been away working in the best interests of Miss Mayer, who owned the chain of shops.

Merle brought in food for him, while Carlos attended the counters and also kept an eye on his personal needs.

As he ate and drank, his stamina was restored. He began to see all that had happened in a better perspective than before. Sooner or later, he knew he was going to have to uproot himself. Probably because Nate had found out the truth and was seeking revenge. He was going to be 'flushed out' and sent on the run again. Maybe Charleen would put two and two together and decide that he was the elusive manager from Clearwater.

Either way, he had to be ready to make a swift move. From the counter-till, he took some wages which were owing to him. Carlos then went over to the livery, paid for services rendered and came back with a fresh horse—a skewbald with a stockingfoot this time—and with Wil's well-used horse jewellery in place.

He talked to Merle and Carlos as he had done so just a few days earlier, told them he had mentioned both of them for a raise in wages, and explained that the private business he had undertaken for the lady proprietor was not yet finished.

'I may return in an hour or two, or I may be away for days. Just keep going. In emergencies, telegraph George Masters. I think you'll find he will understand the situation. So sorry to be elusive, but the other work is imperative. If anyone happens along askin' questions, just tell them I seem to have private problems. Don't mention Miss Mayer because that wouldn't be in her best interests.'

The second parting, although short and totally unexpected, was a cordial one. He rode half a mile down the Newell trail, and presently cut off in a westerly direction. A winding overgrown bear-track took him out to a spot known locally as Trail Fork Rock. This was an age-old outcrop with one point of easy access, and also a precipitous animal-track which gave an alternative route to the eyrie at the summit.

He took the easy way. As soon as he had located the saucer depression on the top, he slackened the skewbald's saddle and turned his attention to the items he had with him. He cleaned his Winchester with infinite care and followed up with an overhaul of his Colt .45.

He had used his spyglass several times by then, but it was a small movement on the Newell trail detected by his naked eye which made him lay aside his equipment and concentrate upon his observations.

Instinct told him he was seeing Charleen forking the big dun with the white blaze. His glass threw her into sharp relief and mildly took his breath away. In a mere day or so, his emotions in regard to that young woman had changed very sharply from how they had been when she was under his father's protection.

She was riding with purposefulness, panache perhaps. Her gaze was set upon the trail in front of her. The brim of her hat curled back due to the pressure of wind resistance. He smiled, and reflected wryly that the Bollard boys were slow at courting. Rich and himself, both.

As he started to think out a way of attracting her attention so that he would not have to make the descent off the outcrop, a part of his mind decided that brother Richard was not worthy of her, even if he turned up and pressed his tentative claims.

FOURTEEN

The flashing of a small round hand-mirror engaged Charlie's attention. After that, Wil did a lot of leaping about with his arms thrown up or outwards, and the girl removed her hat, swishing her bell of copper-tinted hair and beaming at him with her teeth and eyes flashing. He indicated the approach path and went part way down the outcrop to assist her in the ascent.

They were both breathless at the meeting. Wil lowered her gently to the ground and retained a supporting hand and arm about her waist.

Charlie giggled. 'I found out you were a shop-keeper, an' I couldn't keep away.'

'I'm so glad you took the Clearwater trail so soon after our partin', Charlie.

237

Bein' without you didn't seem right. Like I was missin' out on somethin' essential to a full life.'

Breathing hard, Charlie nodded a lot. 'I felt exactly the same way, Wil. We may have entered upon the most foolish venture ever conjured up by man, but havin' started I feel you have to be along with me. This mutual feelin' has to mean something. Maybe we'll live long enough to fully understand it.'

He nodded, and hefted his six-gun which was dragging away at his right thigh. On the top they relaxed completely, dabbing and wiping themselves and smiling shyly at each other.

'Why did you pick this spot to keep watch? Did you know I'd come?'

'I wasn't certain, Charlie. Trail Fork Rock has its advantages. If you didn't come, others might. If you look over the other side, you can make out the trail up from Bitter Creek comin' up through those dwarf pines and drawin' a straightish line through some scrub.'

In a flash, Charlie realised just how concerned Wil was about the Grunbaums and vengeance. 'But you surely wouldn't expect Nate to ride from that direction. Would you?'

'Not exactly. More likely along your back trail. But we can't be too careful. You remember that trick Nate had when he wanted something?'

'You mean shakin' a handful of coins till someone asked what he wanted, an' then gettin' it for him? Yes, I remember that. And a whole lot of other mean tricks, too. But Gail was supposed to send him on to George, in Newell.'

'If he comes, what are we goin' to do, Charlie?'

Charlie stuck her hands on her hips in a provocative pose. 'We're going to retreat, *amigo!* You weren't thinkin' of ambushin' him or anything, were you?'

Wil laughed. He rolled away from Charlie and almost choked on his laughter.

At first, it was in relief that she didn't propose to be separated whatever the odds. And then it was on account of her advocating flight together. He was stuck with her, and it felt good: and, moreover, she was habit-forming as a companion.

Wil had more than an inkling of their special feeling for each other. He was willing to wait for a sure clarification.

Ten minutes later, a small cloud came up the lesser-marked trail from Bitter Creek. It grew, and soon it was possible to pick out four riders. Side by side, intimately close, they watched the riders' progress. There was no immediate need for comment or conversation.

Eventually, Charlie remarked: 'I don't really know how I came to like Nate. Except that he was around, that's all.'

'Don't blame yourself, girl. He could be really amusin' when everythin' was goin' the way he wanted. When he was winnin'. You know how it was. I wonder if four men constitute a huntin' pack?'

Charleen took over the spyglass. She frowned and applied it to her eye. Presently, she whistled. 'Willie Bridson we know about. The other two, they're something again. Men Nate used to call upon. Crease is the one with the dark skin. A breed. A trail-sign reader. And the fourth is Ace Attlebury. Stiff in the saddle. A cutaway coat an' white waistcoat.'

'A tracker and a two-gun man,' Wil interposed. 'Attlebury used to shoot up stray dogs, I recall, an' see off stowaways on the Grunbaum train. A free-loader with a limp died by the bullet. Said to be from Attlebury's gun.'

'They mean business, Wil. We won't stop to explain anything. Make plans. So pleased you stopped me goin' into Clearwater town.'

Wil closed down his spyglass and rolled over, totally out of sight from the trail. 'He's not behavin' like a man who simply wants questions answered, is he? Nate, I mean. We'll wait till they're out of sight, then get down on that trail they came up. I figure we'll cross it and head east, onto the old Circle B territory. We can use one or other of the old line-cabins for a while.'

Charlie nodded. She tied up her hair in the green ribbon, stuck her hat back on her head and awaited the order to get ready. Inwardly, she was thinking that Wil had decided to be hunted on his father's old acreage rather than on territory which he did not know.

She hoped Wil would not be the recipient of a bullet for what he had done to thwart the bridegroom.

One hour later, they paused for refreshment at a line-cabin just inside the eastern perimeter of the old Circle B range. It had a stove, and tinned provisions and other useful items for riders away from towns who needed a meal.

Charleen ate heartily, walking about and talking as she did so.

'Do we wait here, an' look out for pursuit?'

Wil shook his head very decidedly, still chewing. 'No. We go further west. If brother Rich is anywhere around, he'll be the other side of Circle B range, towards the sierras. If we cross the creek an' the railway line I'll feel better.'

'Me, too, Wil. Let me know when you're ready. I could use a swim in the creek.'

Charlie won a swimming race across the creek which had once been poisoned. Wil gave her a start, and assured her by not trying too hard of a victory. He gave her time to recover her breath and practised diving from the surface until she was back on the east bank and partially concealed behind a big towel.

'What time will it be, Wil?'

'Between four an' five in the afternoon! We can rest for a half-hour after we've crossed over, if you like!'

'How long will it take to cross the

railway line an' reach the next cabin?'

'Oh, one hour. Or ninety minutes, provided we don't run into any flocks of sheep. We're well ahead of any possible pursuit yet. So long as no one recognises us along the way.'

The exercise in water took the tension out of them. In a tree stand near the creek bank, Charleen sprawled and dozed while her escort smoked and quietly admired her lissom figure.

Later, they moved on: crossed the railway line which took South Loop traffic and went to earth in the second line-cabin on the western boundary of old Circle B range. Again, they had nothing to trouble them, but both felt inwardly that the time of crisis was not far away.

Shortly after seven o'clock the following morning, Nathan Grunbaum and his escort of three men arrived at the railway track in a bad temper and with his resolve to be revenged on his enemies in no way blunted. He was certain that Charleen and Wilbur had planned his loss of face and nothing would deter him from his own type of showdown.

At the iron way, the four riders paused, already perspiring and impatient: not knowing which way to turn, or whether to ride on, straight across in the hope of picking up a trail which had gone faint during the night. Crease, the tracker, was not very positive, and as Nathan stared into his scarcely blinking eyes, the young Grunbaum felt his pulse-rate mounting.

'All right, *I'll* decide then. We ride south along the line. Cross it at a lower point.'

No one had the nerve to gainsay his pronouncement, and when he came upon three railway workers with a heavy four-wheeled hand-car tightening sections of the track, he beamed sufficiently to show his slightly yellow teeth under his finely trimmed moustache.

'Boys, after gettin' that tip-off in Bitter Creek an' confirmation about Bollard an' that priest's description in Clearwater, I had a feelin' our luck was turnin' sour. But I was wrong. Here we have three hombres drawin' good Grunbaum pay. If they've seen anything, or know anything they'll tell me, an' I won't have to argue. No sir, not with these jaspers.'

The workers in question all wore overalls and bulky peaked caps similar to those used by engineers and fire-boys. They were ill-assorted, and yet their uncomplicated outdoor work suited them and their modest abilities.

Juarez, the lean swarthy Mexican, was the oldest. Previously, he worked in a *cantina*, but as soon as he had tasted liquor himself he became quarrelsome. Ty Waters, a full-faced, fresh-complexioned ex loco engineer, was a few years younger. He had lost face in his previous type of employment after a costly accident. He had worked for the South-Western Pacific railroad company as an engineer. Cy Grunbaum had taken him on, thinking he might come in useful at a later date.

Bo Devlin was the boss of the team; a slow-speaking former cowpuncher who had grown tired of steers. His long nose, fine features and black sideburns belied his thirty-six years, but his bald crown told another tale when he was bareheaded.

Nate called out to the trio, who had looked up from their work.

'What goes on, Bo? I didn't think to find you an' the boys busy this far from town at breakfast-time!'

Bo touched his cap, nodded and grinned. 'Good day to you, Mr Nathan. We had urgent orders from your Pa to check the line, all the way, for slackness. Mr Grunbaum senior is a mite nervous since the big explosion on the main line in the region of North Pass. Happened a couple of days ago, that did.'

Nate cut back on his impatience, and asked another question.

'So how did it happen, this explosion?'

The tone of his voice sounded as if

Devlin might be wholly or partially to blame, but the long-nosed gang boss refused to be put off and merely nodded before proceeding.

'Let me see, it's nearly a month since that hold-up occurred. This time, the dynamite left a big crater. But there was no train due at the time, an' your Pa thinks it was done by amateurs. The track is blown up. The crater is right underneath where the rails were. Of course, it means that a few trips on the flyer will have to be rerouted to this particular loop your family owns. So it can't all be bad.'

Nate spat out a cigar butt. He gave his restless mount a good jab with his rowels and reverted to his habitual scowl.

'You'd know if anything special is due to be moved south, wouldn't you, Bo?'

Devlin nodded hastily and laid a long tobacco-stained finger up the side of his nose. 'Yer, we may be away from town most of the time, but we hear the rumours, Mr Nate. There could be two or maybe three biggish money shipments comin' through. And there's something to do with horse racin' stock, too. Could be a mare and her foal on the move. I guess that might interest you! The biggest shipment might be later today!'

Bridson at once went into a murmured discussion with Crease and Attlebury, but Nate—still angry about being drawn out of town by a false message—refused to be drawn into talk about the racing stock.

'All right, Bo, so you know a lot of interestin' things. But have you, or any of your crew, seen two riders who might have crossed the line in the past few hours? A man an' a woman, we believe. Any signs?'

Waters and Juarez showed great curiosity, but it was clear from the start that none of the trio had seen the elusive couple of riders.

'Nope, Mr Nate,' Bo replied brusquely. 'Me an' my boys, we never seen any riders crossin' the line goin' east or west. Sure is nice to run across you out in the wilds, so to speak. Maybe we'll see you on the way back.'

At that point, the track was on a portion of land slightly built up and not very far from the north-south line of timber in some depth. Hidden in the nearest limits of the self-same timber, Wil Coltman Bollard was able to hear the exchange and also to see who was speaking without benefit of spyglass. He had left Charleen behind, and ventured out alone to reconnoitre the direction from which hostile pursuit might come.

Shortly after arriving in the timber his instinct told him that he himself was being stalked, but he never saw or heard anything to confirm his suspicions, and when the riders and the hand-car workers were in conversation he shrugged off the odd feeling and concentrated upon what he could learn. He was fortunate inasmuch as the animated voice sounds carried with clarity.

As soon as Wil had recovered from the shock of observing the meeting, he began to speculate on Devlin's revelations. Nate was clearly very sensible about having been duped over the foal, but was his interest as deep-rooted as Charleen thought it to be or was ownership of the prestigious animal just a passing fad?

Soon, restlessness claimed the arrogant young rider, and the quartet broke away from the rail track trio and walked their horses still further south before crossing over the permanent way.

FIFTEEN

A belief that to remain free and un-apprehended prompted Wil to remove Charleen from the second line-cabin which had provided shelter for them through the night. Having restocked for a second time, they rode northwards with maximum vigilance and extreme caution. Clearly, Nathan was still hunting them and he had worthwhile knowledge about Wil's scheme to thwart the wedding.

It would take days, possibly weeks even, before the hotheaded young Grunbaum called off the hunt and occupied himself with other rich young men's diversions.

Instinct and a special knowledge of the area ensured that Wil moved in a northerly direction rather than any other. As they rode, towering on the western skyline was the bulky and impressive mountain range, the Sierra del Lobo. Much closer and parallel with the north-south mountain was an overgrown hogsback with the local name of West Ridge.

This same West Ridge was the landmark which drew Wil and his shapely female charge, Charleen. Before and after their long spells away at school, Wilbur and his brother, Richard, had played their boyhood games, tracking each other up and down the animal paths and stalking the slower forms of game with bows and arrows. At times, Nathan Grunbaum had joined them and, slightly less frequently, Charleen had been with them, too.

West Ridge provided a hiding-place of sorts and an observation-point from which riders in thick scrub and foliage could examine the lower terrain towards the east and the railway, and towards the west where the sierra lay.

One third of the way from the southern-most tip, and on the eastern slope under the ridge, Wil and Charlie dismounted and walked their mounts into a shallow hollow screened from the east by long lush fern fronds.

Charleen's dun stood restlessly while she slackened off its harness and bent to give it an overdue grooming. All the time she worked it tossed its head, its white blaze making her blink and stay alert. Five yards away, Wil was similarly busy with the skewbald.

Rolling an unlighted cigar round his mouth, Wil asked: 'Charlie, what are we two doin' right now, scrubbin' away like ostlers in a livery, miles away from anywhere?'

Charlie dabbed away from her brow perspiration which formed all too readily. She chuckled and peered at her partner through a parting in her bell of auburn hair.

'We're keepin' company, Wil, like our folks once expected us to. And workin' towards a common aim, I suppose.

Protectin' each other as far as we can. Are you gettin' tired of my company already?'

'Nope! No, it's not that. Every now an' again I get the feelin' I'll be lucky to have you exclusively to myself. That something will come between us. That all that's happened to our three families recently is unreal! Know what I mean?'

'I know what you mean, Wil. I feel the same way. Come over here, why don't you, an' give me a kiss in case we're about to be interrupted!'

Wil replied: 'Expect me any time.' And then he reflected upon Charlie's words, and his thoughts went back to what he had seen earlier in the timber, and that strange feeling that he was not alone. But he shrugged it away, and complied eagerly with his superior girl rider's wishes.

A reaction ran through his blood, coursing through his whole being. He crushed her in his embrace and gradually revolved her through a half-circle. One hundred and eighty degrees on, he reacted for the first time to what his eyes were telling him. Charlie had her back to a gap in the ferns, and through that same gap something untoward was happening.

Several small plumes of smoke topped an area ringed in by stones at plain level. And within the ring were perhaps twelve or more riders, all dismounted and taking their ease. Charlie became aware of the slackening pressure of Wil's embrace. At first, it was a relief: it helped with her breathing. Later, she knew something had taken his attention. Probably something of a serious nature.

'What—what is it, Wil?' she whispered.

He shook his head. As she disentangled herself from his arms, the direction of his gaze became clear.

'Company of some sort. Down there. In the hollow. Between this ridge an' the railroad track. Many men. And horses.'

Once again, they crouched side by side, and stared. Wil lighted his cigar with a lithe familiar movement.

'Is it a posse of some sort, Wil?'

His shoulders moved upwards. 'Business of some sort. Legal or illegal. It could be outlaws, I suppose. Maybe it's something to do with rerouted trains, an' what they carry.'

The girl slipped away and returned with the spyglass. Her hand was a little unsteady as she handed it over to Wil. He placed it to his eyes, and hurriedly adjusted the space between the ends.

'Twelve, maybe thirteen men in view. No signs of peace officers' stars anywhere. Nobody we know. That's a relief, I suppose.'

Charlie took the glass without answering him. She was not quite sure about how he came to be relieved. Using his focus, she lined up the glass and studied what he had already seen. A sudden restlessness on the part of the mounts should have warned them that all was not well, but the intriguing scene below held their attention.

The blow which struck Wil on the back of the head was administered by the barrel of a .44 Colt. Charleen partially stifled a scream, as her partner groaned and slowly toppled forward, off-balance, losing consciousness. She turned, holding the spyglass like a weapon, but the assailant's casual handling of the revolver assured her that she stood no chance of fighting against him.

The gun barrel indicated in which direction she should move while Wil was subjected to a close scrutiny. The assailant was an agile, stocky man wearing an old confederacy army tunic and the sort of wide-brimmed campaign hat worn by General Robert E Lee's cavalry. A white bandanna hid the lower part of the face. Only a pair of restless brown eyes showed, apart from the straight black brows and matching hair at the temples.

His laugh was offputting, and yet it was familiar. As he snatched away his mask, Charleen gasped with surprise. She was seeing the tight, turned-down full lips and Syrian nose of Wil's brother, Richard. And yet there was no sign of friendliness. Rich's smile as a grown-up had always been a mocking one. On this occasion, it seemed to have become a permanent acquisition.

'Fancy meetin' *you* here, Mrs Grunbaum. And my dear, long-lost brother, Wilbur, of all people. Hidin' away up here, avoidin' your husband, an' keepin' watch on a group of my friends who would be very upset if they knew you were observing them.'

Wil, on his hands and knees, slowly recovered consciousness. He arrested his whirling vision to focus on his brother, and his immediate thoughts began to assemble.

'So it was *you*, Rich! You were down in the timber beside the track when Nate stopped to question the hand-car gang!'

'And why shouldn't I have been down there, big brother? After all, I still have business in these parts. That's more than you can say. I can't say I approve of you runnin' off with old Nate's new bride like this, though.'

He twisted the spyglass out of Charleen's hand and stood with his feet apart. In his black boots, his stance was not unlike that of the Emperor Napoleon's as he lifted the spyglass and peered through it. While he was busy, Wil removed his hat and dabbed the back of his head. This time his skull was only bruised. There was no cut or blood visible.

'If only you'd been around to marry Charlie, here, like we all expected, none of our present troubles would ever have arisen!'

Wil's words sounded like a condemnation. He provoked an instant reaction from his brother, who turned on the two of them.

'You fool! She was never interested in me. It was Nate an' his latest horse. Nate an' the family private coach. Nate an' his new shootin' irons. Nate *always! Never* Richard! So don't try an' con me about where Charleen's affections were supposed to go. She was Nathan's, always. I said you were a fool, an' I'll say it again, Wil. Only a fool would run off with her, *after* the wedding had taken place!'

'She's not married to him, Rich,' Wil argued, rising unsteadily to his feet. 'The real parson failed to turn up. I took his place. That's why I'm bein' hunted by Nate, right now.'

Rich was thoughtful. He spat at Wil's feet and sneered. 'What a brother. You mishandled the spread, sold off the stock, drank and gambled away the profits, an' now you want me to believe you stood in for a priest! Well, you can save your words, because she's still wearing Nathan's ring.'

For several seconds, there was virtual silence. Wil and Charleen had both forgotten the significance of the ring: had forgotten that Charlie still had it on her finger. They were stunned. Obviously, Rich had not heard anything about the pseudo-priest. He had been too busy going to earth between towns.

First Wil tried to explain. Then Charleen did the same. Rich was impatient, and utterly disinterested. He had no warm feelings left for either his former girlfriend, or his brother. He had grown used to thwarting the law, and ill-using anyone who too long stayed in his way.

'Save your breath, you two. I'm takin' you down to meet those hombres you were spyin' on. Whether she's married or not, they'll be keen to make her acquaintance on account of some unfinished business which might just go wrong.'

Standing side by side with their hands on their heads, Wil and Charlie wondered fearfully about his latest unexpected development.

'Rich, a lot of what you said about my earlier behaviour was right. I deserved kickin'. I'm sorry I let you down when I was supposed to run things an' protect you. Did you ever find out who it was poisoned the creek on Circle B range?'

The younger Bollard ignored the last question. 'All right, so you're sorry. Now stay still there till I get my horse. If you attempt any foolish escape tricks I'll hogtie the pair of you before we ride off. Is that understood?'

Rich took their weapons. Within five minutes, all three—mounted—were headed down the side of the hogsback on a narrow animal track. It was so steep in places that any attempt to cut and run could have precipitated a nasty accident.

Wil led the way. He felt that Charlie, close behind him, was seeing him in a very bad light. And Rich's truthful accusations were bound to affect the girl's future attitude to him. He found himself wondering if Nate would part with a big ransom for Charleen, in the event that kidnap was added to the other crime or crimes at this time brewing in the valley below.

Nearing the lower level, Rich decided to talk.

'These hombres I'm takin' you to. You shouldn't do anything to upset them. They're very keen. Just the other day a small explosion turned into a big one, because they used too much dynamite. And it went off too early, of course. I'd say they'll get the operation right this time, though, workin' on the south loop. Only thing is, I can't predict how they behave towards ladies. Only time will tell the answer to that one.'

Wil felt sick at heart. He knew that his younger brother was capable of causing anyone he knew heartache, but Charlie was a mighty attractive proposition and she might become an unwilling diversion for men intent upon train robbery.

He called over his shoulder: 'Hey, Rich, you listen to me. I've made it my business to keep Charleen under Bollard protection. You're still a Bollard, even if you thwart the law. If anything happens to me, Charlie's safety will be down to you!'

Rich yawned. 'I hear you, big brother, an' I'm not impressed. The two of you are only survivors because you might become useful to my partners in adverse circumstances. Take my advice, don't do too much arguin' when we get there. Okay?'

Five minutes later, hidden rifles clicked on either side of the approaching mounted trio. Rich announced who he was, and the guards showed themselves. Countless ribald remarks drifted around the hollow as the two prisoners were put in the middle and helped to dismount.

The leader, a big fellow with a chin beard and knife scar near his left eye, welcomed them with a big gesture. He had a red scarf across the top of his head instead of a hat. At times, earlier wounds gave him head pains which made a hat unbearable.

Grudgingly, Charleen allowed him to take her hand. 'Hey, hey, that's a pretty bauble, my dear. Tell you what, I'll trade my earring for it, one for one! What do you say?'

Charleen declined to reply, but Rich saw his chance to add fuel to the situation. 'Her husband, Nathan Grunbaum, son of the South Loop's owner, gave her that ring. So it ought to be worth a few hundred dollars, boys. It surely ought to be removed, if she's ever ransomed. What do you say?'

Loud banter showed the rest of the gang were impressed, but their approval seemed to be short-lived. Rich introduced his big brother, and the peculiar atmosphere was heightened, as vicious, suspicious, greed-motivated men looked from one Bollard to the other.

Wil wondered if his brother was mistrusted, but he thrust the thought aside as being merely wishful thinking. He wondered, as well, which of his enemies was the most deadly.

SIXTEEN

Wil and Charleen were placed in a freshly fashioned dugout, cut into the east side of the hollow. In spite of Wil's protests, Charlie received the same treatment as himself. They were trussed by the ankles and wrists, with a linking rope to keep their arms and legs behind them. One body in one corner, the second in another. Right from the start they were embarrassed to be in each other's company in such a humiliating way.

For a minute or so, a contest developed about who could wriggle the most, but neither of them made any headway with their bonds.

Charleen whimpered and took Wil's attention.

'What is it, love? Have you given yourself

a rope burn?'

Putting on a brave face, the girl shook her head. 'It's not that. A small worm, or a grub of some sort, fell from the ceiling. It went down my shirt. Don't—take any notice of me, Wil. I'm feelin' sorry for myself.'

Outside, in the open, the outlaws gathered around their leader, the bearded Fournier, and Rich Bollard. There was no door on the dugout. Only a canvas cover separated the prisoners from their captors.

'Let's not forget what it was you went out to discover, Bollard. We haven't heard yet.'

Rich Bollard waited for silence. 'I was able to get close enough to overhear a conversation between three men operatin' on the line from a hand-car. They were talkin' to Nate Grunbaum an' three others. Grunbaum was told there were two or three biggish shipments of money comin' through. The crew man said the biggest shipment might be later today, an' he knew about the mare an' foal bein' moved, too.'

'Did he say what time it would be through?'

'No, he didn't mention the time, but we already know it to within a half-hour, so it doesn't matter, Jacques.'

There was a flurry of questions and answers which sounded as if it would develop into a full-scale discussion. Just when the voices were at their loudest, Fournier raised his own strident voice and cut them short.

'You're goin' over old ground. It's time we were on our way, an' you know it. I want those two prisoners gagged, an' their horses stripped an' put into the park over there.'

Two evil-looking men moved into the dugout and saw to the gags. Wil did not have time to protest, this time. A minute or two later, the familiar sounds of men mounting horses carried to the prisoners.

One of the villains squeezed Charleen's thigh before retiring, but nothing could be done about it. Wil strained against his bonds and merely brought tears to his eyes. Breathing was not as easy as it should have been.

Amid the gasping, the sound of which filled the whole dugout when the outlaws had left, Charleen contrived to get to her knees, but she lost her balance and tipped over, breast downward, bumping her head and losing her hat.

Wil's blood-pressure appeared to increase, and he had to keep quite still for a while so as not to choke. His ears sang, so that neither he nor Charlie heard the eventual departure of the would-be train robbers.

Five minutes were used up by the time Wil had crossed to Charlie's corner moving an inch or two at a time on his knees. After that, he contrived to shuffle in behind her, crab-like. He lost a lot of perspiration and his limbs ached, but he made it. He used her shoulder to remove his stetson. As it rolled clear, he turned over so that his face was towards her. Charlie trembled, not fully aware of what he was trying to do.

At the back of her head where the gag was secured, the knot moved over her smooth tresses. Wil worked it down to her neck, using his nose and drawing from it a slight trickle of blood before he achieved the success he worked for.

Charlie arched her back still more and tucked in her chin, until she was able to slip clear of the gag by working her lower jaw. She licked the corners of her mouth, removing tiny traces of blood. Although it was painful at first, she contrived to give him a full smile. Only his eyes could reply to her winning ways.

'I know what's the matter with me, Wil. I'm in love. I love you, Wil.'

She thought she knew what his painful nod indicated, but she did not waste any time. Using her teeth, she picked and bit upon the knots of his gag until he, too, was able to breathe freely and talk. His lungs were still labouring when he answered.

'I love you too, Charlie. I have a feelin' bein' with you is makin' a man out of me. All the same, I don't feel I can break out without your help. Even though there's a black-handled knife stickin' in the roof timbers.'

Charleen gasped, and followed his gaze. It appeared to be a worn blade with a dark wooden handle, left there when the dugout was being fashioned.

Wil spat out bits of cotton. 'Where do I get the strength to clamber up on that table an' reach for the knife with my back arched like an acrobat's?'

'I could work on the rope holdin' your arms back, but it would take longer than the gag.'

'I'll not have your mouth hurt any more an' that's my rulin'!'

Charleen smiled and licked her mouth corners once more. She gave him the incentive by three powerful kisses, although it took a lot of concentrated effort to get in a position for mouth to mouth kissing.

After that, it was a long slow effort. Wil made it onto a low bench first, using his knees. Next, he struggled to the higher level of the table-top. Rough splinters probed the skin over his knees as he tugged out the knife with his teeth.

Actually sawing at the ropes pinioning Charlie's wrists was a long energy-sapping ordeal, which did little to boost Wil's morale. When she finally announced her hands were loose, the knife slithered from his fingers and he pitched forward, needing above all other considerations to ease the aches in his back.

Charlie dabbed him carefully and lovingly, and waited until he had recovered a little before sawing at his bonds with all her remaining energies and a lot of patience. Eventually, he burst the last few strands by hauling against the top of the bench.

Five more agonising minutes elapsed before they were both free.

The chafing of sore limbs was a labour of love. Presently, Wil stood up and walked about. He crossed to the door, and found out that no guard had been posted. Next, he collected their two hats. Before he restored Charlie's to its rightful spot, he took her comb and used it on her long tresses with infinite care.

'This is decision time, Charlie.' They seated themselves on the benches, one either side of the table, and held hands. 'It seems to me we have two or three alternatives. You want I should outline my notions?'

Charleen nodded. 'But first let's get the obvious thing out of the way. Whatever we do, we do it together. Right?'

'Right, Charlie.' They sealed that agreement with a kiss. 'So, we could recover our mounts an' cautiously slip away to westward. Disappear over the Sierra del Lobo, if you feel like it.'

'I do feel like it, Wil, but I don't think we're goin' to do it, are we? If we are bent on helping law an' order, we'd have to ride after the outlaws an' seek to alert the train crew. How about that?'

'It may lead to shootin', an' that's dangerous. Is it worth the risk?'

'Even if we avoid the hold-up issue, Nate an' his boys may get close enough to aim bullets at us!'

'All right then, after the outlaws it is. Maybe Nate will be kind of us if we try to save the payroll an' the livestock!'

The saddling took a good ten minutes time. All the minutes they were busy they talked, discussing exactly what they planned to do. At last, they were ready. Instinct made Wil head for the north, with West Ridge bulking up on their left. In the first mile, there was little to suggest that they were on the right track. However, they were never far from the permanent way and that gave them some confidence.

At the top of a sharp rise which had their horses blowing a little he reined in. Charleen came up with him, and at once her keen green eyes picked out the incongruous heap of wood stacked across the rails a hundred or so yards ahead of them at a lower level.

'There's a block of ties, Wil, so I guess Fournier an' Rich an' the others are somewhere below us, flankin' the rails. Maybe we're just in time.'

Wil dismounted and encouraged Charlie to do the same. As he did so, he marvelled at the calmness of her voice. She talked as if a clash with outlaws was an everyday event. He surveyed the railside rocks for sign of hostiles, while the girl did the same with her naked eye.

'They've picked a good spot, Charlie. A loaded train will be movin' up that grade at a slow speed. Whatever happens, it ain't goin' to be pretty.'

By the time he was ready to hand over the glass, Charlie had her Henry rifle out of the saddle scabbard and checked over for immediate use. He undid his bandanna, made a pad of it and instructed her to place it under her shirt to protect her shoulder.

After snagging the reins over a tree branch, Wil headed her forward a few yards to where a large flat-topped boulder gave cover and provided a rest for their weapons.

'Don't take any chances, Charlie. We fire for the loco's tank, if it shows up.'

'I understand, Wil. After that, though, we may have to aim at the outlaws, just to protect ourselves.'

While they agreed Rich would have to take his chance, the first sounds of a distant locomotive came across the rarefied air over the old cattle range. Oddly enough, the long-awaited sounds made hiding men show themselves who had previously remained discreetly hidden. Fournier's men were in small groups, some fifty yards past the wooden barrier, half on the west side and half on the east.

Two minutes later, the locomotive appeared distantly, coming round a bend near the bottom of the grade. Thick black smoke billowed up from its huge smoke-stack to slowly disperse towards the north-west.

Wil called: 'This is it, partner!'

'Good luck, partner,' Charlie called back.

Wil's first ranging shot with the Winchester actually clipped the tall chimney without doing much damage. The noise made by the loco drowned out the sound of the gunshot. Wil levered and aimed again. Charlie fired just ahead of him. Both their bullets hit the front of the boiler. A scowling face appeared at one of the small round look-out windows in the cab. The expression changed. The head withdrew.

A flurry of four shots hit the front of the rock behind which Wil and Charlie were sheltered. Wil ducked and Charlie flinched. Now, they were involved. Chips of stone and ricochets made life hazardous. Abruptly, Wil pulled Charlie down, till they were both kneeling. His arms encircled her protectively, almost roughly.

'Aren't you afraid the outlaws may catch us unprepared?' the girl whispered.

'Not yet a while, they won't,' Wil advised her. 'Don't forget they're motivated by greed!'

For a short while, the early exchanges between the outlaws and the protective guns on the train appeared to be muted. In time, the spurious silence alerted them. They rose slowly to their feet without disengaging.

SEVENTEEN

While Wil and Charlie cautiously observed the booming gun battle, the two groups took stock of each other and each saw that the other would take a lot of stopping. The outlaws, who had planned to gain access to the cars after shooting one or two defenders to frighten the remainder suddenly became aware that the train carried men with rifles, specially put aboard to protect the cash and other valuables.

Neither side showed any sign of weakening: nor did anyone make decisive progress.

'I'd say there's a sheriff on board, with sworn deputies, but even so they need help to dislodge the men in the rocks. Do you agree, Charleen?'

'I do, Wil. Let's find a better spot and put some bullets among them.'

Almost at once, the observers were in action. No one was seen to be wounded or killed, but the way the lead sailed in and ricocheted made them feel their additional fire was helpful. More bullets came from the train on the near side, and yet the train defenders did not gain the advantage. Other outlaws, operating on the other side prevented progress being made.

Wil and his partner kept up their intermittent shooting for nearly five minutes. As they felt their weapons grow hot, and wondered if they were wasting ammunition, a new development took place. Acting in haste, three men hauled a gatling machine-gun onto an open platform at the rear of the second carriage and hurriedly lined it upon the railside rocks.

A retaliatory flurry held up the gatling's action for a few seconds, but a few timely shots from Wil made it possible for a brave man to put the superior weapon into the struggle. As its staccato tune echoed up the hillside, Wil began to feel relieved.

'Sure is lucky they thought to have a proper defensive force on board, Charlie, girl,' Wil called hoarsely.

Charleen moved closer, resting her chin on his shoulder and taking confidence from his presence. 'Unless my eyesight is suffering, I'd say the rearmost wagon is slipping away from the rest! What does that mean?'

Through the spyglass, Wil studied it closely. 'It's one of those solid trucks used for transportin' horses. Probably, the foal an' the mare will be in there. That's if they're with this train. Why don't we make a detour, go after the truck?'

Once again, Charlie agreed without hesitation. They mounted up once more and began to make their way downgrade, keeping well back from the area of the railside rocks and staying on the alert. The continued exchanges, mostly between the train's defenders and the outlaws on the other side, reminded the riders where the action was, and helped them to check their progress.

The horse-wagon had gone out of sight, its progress boosted by the downgrade. Wil, however, had a clear idea as to how far it might run of its own accord before the terrain levelled out. He explained his findings to Charleen and they continued to ride with all speed.

Behind them, the sheriff had decided to swing his gatling gun away from the targets to westward and instead fire on the attackers on the east side. As it happened, Fournier, the bearded leader with the earring and facial scar, anticipated the sheriff's move.

'Fall back, men! Get mounted up. It's time to switch to that second plan to do with the mare an' foal. Besides, we have no answer to that gatling which took out our buddies on the other side. Move with caution!'

As if to underline the latest advice, the gatling started to spit bullets in their direction. At first, they flew too high, but soon the gunner brought down the barrel and put his lethal projectiles in among the rocks. A whole magazine was fired off before it came clear that the ambushers had changed their strategy. And still the firing went on.

Furthest from the flying bullets was Rich Bollard. Over the years he had become ruthless, greedy and self-seeking. He, it was, who had contrived a chance to uncouple the rearmost box with the dire warning for unauthorised personnel to keep out.

Having slipped the coupling, he had clung to the side by hanging onto a vertical iron ladder which gave access to the roof. At the outset, he had discovered that the sliding door used to get horses in and out was secured on the inside. Although this precaution frustrated him, it added to his confident belief that he had within his grasp the renowned mare named Cascade and her hopefully awaited foal, to be called Flying Spray.

At the bottom of the grade, the wagon was slow to lose speed. Rich's limbs ached. It was still moving slowly when he began his ascent, hampered by his rifle and the two revolvers at his waist. A quick glance around assured him that no one was close enough to shoot him while he made his search. He stood up, crossed the rounded roof, pulled up the trapdoor and stuck his head into the opening, eagerly peering downwards for his first glimpse of the priceless animal.

There were no quadrupeds in there, at all. No horses. Nothing. Only empty stalls, a few discarded items of harness and hay feed.

He had schemed from the start to outwit everybody and get the biggest reward for himself, exclusively. Now, he realised that the authorities had outthought the renegades. And, consequently, he was outfaced the most.

Much closer than the approaching group ramrodded by Fournier, he could hear horses. A slight panic cut through his mounting anger and made him look around carefully. Somewhere off into the trees, east of the wagon; possibly a smaller group of riders, acting independently of all those in action so far. They were not close enough for him to identify Nathan Grunbaum and his sidekicks.

Far, far nearer than the group not in sight, and approaching the wagon speedily from the south-west were two other riders known to him. His excellent eyesight soon revealed who they were. His brother, Wil Bollard, and that bitch, Charleen Mayer, so recently married to Cy Grunbaum's spoiled brat, Nate. He sighed, and spat on the roof.

'Hell an' tarnation, I've missed out all day. No share in the payroll. No mare an' no foal. No horse to ride off on. Unless—unless I shoot up my beloved brother, also the runaway bride. That way,

I'll be the only Bollard still breathin' an' I'll have useful ridin' stock to speed my getaway.'

He started to laugh. His dryness made his merriment almost soundless, like the panting of a dog.

Wil reined in to warn Charleen of a dangerous sudden dip. They were side by side when a parting in the foliage gave them their first true clear view of the prone figure on the wagon roof. Wil leaned over and grabbed Charlie's reins.

'That's brother Rich. I don't like it.'

Charlie whistled. 'My eyes again? I'd swear he's got a rifle lined up on us!'

Before they could react further, the brief flame at the muzzle of the shoulder weapon showed that it had been fired. The first bullet flew. Rich levered, and fired again. And a further bullet.

The first missile struck Wil's saddlehorn and narrowly missed his ribs. He was attempting to get Charlie to flatten herself along the dun's neck when the unfortunate animal absorbed a bullet in a vital spot. It started to fold up almost at once. Charlie gasped. She pitched over its shoulder and went head first down the tricky incline, brushing sharp plants and bruising twigs before her fall ended in an eight-foot pit.

Unaware that his bandanna had been singed, Wil slid to the ground and scrambled down the slope after her with his spur wheels protesting all the way. The dying dun made a sideways somersault with flying flailing legs, until life failed it and its body came to rest. At the top of the pit, Wil hovered. Somehow, he had drawn his Winchester from the scabbard as he cleared leather. He was angry as he shouted into the hole.

'My brother, Rich, is insane. He could have killed you. I'm goin' to settle with him whether you are alive or not alive, Charlie, an' I don't want you to argue with me on this one.'

He was stunned. He knew his utterances

had not altogether made sense. She was face down. Crumpled. Not in any ungainly shape. Just hurt. She moved a little, felt herself over and turned so that her scratched face was visible to him.

'How—how are you, Charlie, my love?'

'Bruised, shaken, scratched. Weak. But no bones broken, I think. My horse is dead?'

Wil nodded. He licked his dry lips. His anger was justified. Rich had turned them over to outlaws one time. This time, he had fired a rifle to kill. He wanted to argue with Charleen, but she did not offer him the makings.

'Come back for me, love, if Rich is the first priority, I'll be all right. You'll see.'

Wil nodded again. 'I won't be long, I promise you.'

He drew his Colt and slid it down the side of the pit. Charleen took charge of it. Unspoken messages passed between them. Eventually, Wil stood up and left her with great reluctance.

Two hundred yards of the railway line, opposite the spot where the last wagon had come to rest, Grunbaum, Bridson, Attlebury and Crease reined in on a slight ridge and began to take stock of what they could see. The recent firing of weapons had drawn them in the direction of the railway. It was clear by the volume of fire, and the protracted nature of the exchanges, that a substantial strike was being made against the train.

The last wagon clearly had some special significance, with the prone gunman crouched on the roof, his gun still smoking from the muzzle. Attlebury, however, had a spyglass trained up the grade.

'Looks like a loco, a tender, a mail van, and four carriages back there. The defenders appear to have stood off a determined assault. And there's a line of riders headin' through the lower timber, comin' this way. Maybe headed for this particular wagon!'

Bridson grabbed the glass and took a look, confirming what Attlebury had quoted, but Nate already had his mind made up.

'I can guess what's in that wagon. It'll be the mare, Cascade, an' the foal, Flyin' Spray. If we take charge, I can be almost sure of gettin' the foal for myself. But we'll have to hurry, otherwise this renegade outfit will get there first, an' they'll outnumber us.'

Crease cleared his throat. 'The man on the roof is one called Rich Bollard, who used to hang around South Loop an' these parts. Younger of the old rancher's boys.'

Nate nodded, and lined up his rifle. 'He's got it comin'. Back me up, boys. Then stand by to take over the wagon.'

Nate fired and missed. Rich rolled hurriedly to one side, and wondered how to counter the new threat. Three further bullets hit the upper parts of the wagon before he came up with an idea. He waved the barrel of the rifle, making a signal.

'Hold your fire! Don't shoot, you'll hit the mare or the foal if you do. Come over if you're interested.'

The flurry of gunfire faded. Rich rose to one knee. In two or three minutes Fournier and his boys would be along, and then he would be comparatively safe. Slowly, he rose to his feet. As he did so, a voice floated up to him from the other side.

'You shouldn't have fired on Charleen, Rich. A Bollard who would do that doesn't deserve to live! This is it!'

No time for protest, Wil fired, levered, fired again, and levered once more. His aim was accurate. The first bullet hit Rich in the shoulder. The second went through his ribs, left side, as he sank to his knees. He was dying as he collapsed and slipped off the roof, plunging to rail level. Three or four rifles fired by Fournier's men probed for Wil's position, but he was already withdrawing, being far more interested in Charlie and her condition than anything his enemies were due to seize or cede.

Hurriedly the Grunbaum contingent dismounted, found defensive positions and took on the five or six outlaws still in business. Spasmodic shooting marked their position and their progress, or the lack of it for quite a time.

Charlie came up on the end of a lariat, shaken and scratched but otherwise still complete. The sight of her dead mount distressed her, but she was not slow to mount up behind Wil whose expression told her all she needed to know about the recent clash with brother Rich.

Purely by chance, the tiring skewbald—headed in the direction most likely to be peaceful—led them into the path of a large party of riders grouped about a sizeable horse-box on wheels. Inscribed on the side of it was the name of the owner, *Luke Rottenberg,* and his main purpose in life, *Horse breeder.*

In fact, the senior Rottenberg was there himself. His party was made up of men from his own outfit and others from a country-wide organisation who hired out guards.

Wil touched his hat, explained who Charleen was, and also described as much as he knew about the recent clashes between outlaws and the train. Rottenberg turned out to be keen, but courteous. He alerted his outer ring of guns about the wagon which really did contain the mare, Cascade, and the new foal, Flying Spray, and supplied Charleen with a spare horse. He also offered protection for as far as Wil and Charleen cared to ride with him, headed—as he was—for the county to the south of Hot Springs.

The knowledge that so many people, honest and dishonest, had been successfully duped about how the mare and foal were being transported, put the Rottenberg party in high good humour. Although it did not become clear right away, the groups exchanging gun-shots eventually tired of testing each other and rode off in opposite directions. The ties were cleared and the train moved on towards its destination without anyone bothering immediately to retrieve the wayward wagon.

At last, Wil and Charleen had time to discuss their future plans which were easy to put together.

'At the first town over the county line, we could talk about gettin' married,' Wil suggested. 'Such a move would encourage friend Nathan to abandon all hope in that direction.'

'A bold, but practical plan, *amigo,*' Charleen replied, approvingly. 'We'd have no necessity to return to South Loop in a hurry, but I could send back Nate's ring to him by messenger, of course. It'll be interestin' to return to South Loop as Mrs Bollard. And there are other considerations.'

Irrelevantly, Wil remarked: 'You know I figure I ought to shave off my beard and moustache before we alert the parson.

What other considerations did you have in mind?'

'Why, the business of visiting each and every branch of the South-Western Traders to explain to all the managers that the owner has changed, but in name only.'

Wil fished out his last small cigar, which was bent. He lighted it and sucked on it with obvious satisfaction. He murmured: 'Mrs Charleen Bollard. I like it. I guess I could make the trip around the shops with you. We could look upon it as a honeymoon, if you like. What do you say?'

'I say, *si, amigo.*' They rode on with hands linked, totally unembarrassed.

The publishers hope that this book has given you enjoyable reading. Large Print Books are especially designed to be as easy to see and hold as possible. If you wish a complete list of our books, please ask at your local library or write directly to: Dales Large Print Books, Long Preston, North Yorkshire, BD23 4ND, England.

Other DALES Western Titles In Large Print

ELLIOT CONWAY
The Dude

JOHN KILGORE
Man From Cherokee Strip

J. T. EDSON
Buffalo Are Coming

ELLIOT LONG
Savage Land

HAL MORGAN
The Ghost Of Windy Ridge

NELSON NYE
Saddle Bow Slim

Other DALES Western Titles In Large Print

BILL WADE
Dead Come Sundown

JIM CLEVELAND
Colt Thunder

AMES KING
Death Rides The Thunderhead

NELSON NYE
The Marshal Of Pioche

RAY HOGAN
Gun Trap At Arabella

BEN BRIDGES
Mexico Breakout

This Large Print Book for the Partially sighted, who cannot read normal print, is published under the auspices of

THE ULVERSCROFT FOUNDATION

THE ULVERSCROFT FOUNDATION

. . . we hope that you have enjoyed this Large Print Book. Please think for a moment about those people who have worse eyesight problems than you . . . and are unable to even read or enjoy Large Print, without great difficulty.

You can help them by sending a donation, large or small to:

The Ulverscroft Foundation, 1, The Green, Bradgate Road, Anstey, Leicestershire, LE7 7FU, England.

or request a copy of our brochure for more details.

The Foundation will use all your help to assist those people who are handicapped by various sight problems and need special attention.

Thank you very much for your help.